UNTWISTED
Cari Quinn & Taryn Elliott
Lost In Oblivion: Book 2.5

UNTWISTED

*Falling in love was easy...figuring out the rhythm of being a couple,
not so much.*

Now that they've pressed play, life is going way too fast for
Gray Duffy and Jazz Edwards. A super hot video has boosted
their band Oblivion's popularity even higher, and suddenly Gray
and Jazz are the reigning prince and princess of rock. But as their
private wedding ceremony in their most special place approaches,
they realize they can't go forward without facing their roots.

With new family members coming into the mix and old
unresolved dramas coming to a head, one thing is for sure—the
harder they rock, the bigger the drop.

COPYRIGHT

DEDICATION

To my mom, who cheerleads without words more than she knows.
To Taryn Elliott, who is always there at the eleventh hour and all the hours in between.

CHAPTER ONE

The innocuous pale blue envelope sat on the table between Jazz and Harper. A smiley face sticker had been placed in one corner beside the recipient's name and address, which had been written in bright purple ink.

Jasmine Edwards c/o Ripper Records.

The sender? Molly McIntire. The little sister Jazz hadn't seen in a decade.

If it really was Molly at all.

"Interesting that it's not made out to Jazz," Harper said, folding her hands on her small baby bump. She was a couple of months farther along than Jazz and had that whole glowing thing going on, as evidenced by the rosiness of her cheeks and sparkle in her eye.

At least her eyes has been sparkling until Jazz asked her to meet for an emergency lunch at the Mexican restaurant near their apartment. Harper was about to move out of the place the members of Jazz's band, Oblivion—Nick, Simon, Gray and Deacon—shared. Lucky Harper and her sexy manster of a husband Deacon had bought a little place in the Valley and were jumping ship.

They weren't the only ones. Jazz glanced down at her engagement ring. Gray had mentioned just last week that he thought they should try to find a place of their own before the baby came in the fall.

Their baby, not Harper and Deacon's baby. And no, contrary to what Nick had speculated, they had not added fertility drugs to the water in the Hollywood Hills. It was just coincidence.

Getting this letter now might be another one. *Might.*

"Molly didn't call me Jazz. She was a little girl when I...left." A nice way to refer to being tossed out on her ear and put into foster care. "She called me 'Mine', because she had trouble with Jasmine when she was a baby. I remember her standing in her crib crying for me, just saying 'Mine' over and over again. The name stuck." Jazz smiled and sipped her iced tea. She probably should cut back on the caffeine but she figured her once a day iced tea couldn't hurt that much. "My mom didn't understand she meant me."

"What did the letter say? Does it seem authentic?"

"I don't know. I haven't opened it yet."

Harper sighed and pushed cheese off her burrito. "What does Gray think?"

"I haven't had a chance to talk to him." And she wasn't bummed about that at all. Surely she could get through a whole day without having a crisis she absolutely had to discuss with her best friend. Her best friend who just happened to now be her fiancé.

"How come?"

"He had a big meeting with a producer today and he was distracted last night, thinking the guy wouldn't like his stuff."

Gray being distracted was a usual thing since he'd come back from rehab. At first she'd figured he was still trying to get used to not being at the facility any longer, but then she'd begun to realize that in the eight weeks he'd been gone, he'd developed a new obsession. He stayed up late almost every night, writing and playing his guitar. That wasn't unusual. But how driven he was to produce new material was.

They had a wedding to plan, a house to buy and a baby on the way. He had debts to pay back. And evidently he needed to take care of all of those things right this very second.

"Are you okay?" Harper leaned forward. "This letter really has you rattled."

There was no use in pretending otherwise. "Yeah. It does."

"And you haven't been able to talk about it with Gray, and that has you twice as messed up." Harp took her hand. "I get it. I'm the same way with the big guy. It's gotta be even worse since you've been confiding in him so long."

"He's just busy. I get it. He's trying to be the daddy, you know?" She laughed and poked at her rice with her fork, although she wasn't that hungry. Shocking enough in itself, since her kid had proven to be a marathon eater already.

"He wants to make sure everything is taken care of financially. You know how it is, our money isn't always consistent and we're not sure when we're getting what." Harp nodded and released her, and Jazz dropped her hand in her lap with a sigh. "Plus, he thinks he needs to pay me and his parents back as fast as humanly possible for the Cricket situation, although I've told him fifty times my money is his. He's just too stubborn to listen."

"A stubborn man? No way. I've never encountered one of those."

Jazz grinned. Talking to Harper always evened her out. "So I guess I should open the letter, huh? No reason to freak out until I see what it says." She ran the edge of one of her purple fingernails along the envelope. "Maybe she's telling me to never bother her and she wants no contact."

Harp snorted. "Somehow I doubt it. More likely she wants to shake you down for some cash."

"What? Why would you think that?"

"Honey, you're famous now. Gads, you're even *more* famous now since that vid of you and Gray setting the bed on fire has been plastered everywhere."

Jazz ducked her head and hoped like hell she wasn't actually blushing. She was a grown woman. So they'd made out in a video for a really dirty song about oral sex. A song Gray had written about eating her out. Big deal. People did that every day, right?

Their child would probably be horrified in a decade or so, but by then maybe no one would even remember the vid anymore.

Except Gray, who claimed it was the best not-a-porno he'd ever seen.

"I wouldn't say famous exactly," Jazz began.

"I would," Harper replied flatly. "Your name is everywhere right now. You guys just had an interview in Rolling Stone, for God's sake."

"It wasn't an interview," Jazz protested. "Just an itty bitty column about the video and the producers who want to work with Gray."

Everyone seemed to all of a sudden. Once Lila had put the word out on the street that Gray been instrumental in writing Oblivion's first big hit, "The Becoming," and that he'd penned the bulk of their extremely buzzed about new single, "Sugar Kiss," he'd become LA's new It guy. And he was taking full advantage, working his ass off.

Working too much, if she was honest. He'd just finished up his part of recording on their upcoming album "Rise" that he'd missed while he was in rehab, and that time in the studio had meant lots of late nights. She'd hung out with him a lot of the time despite her sections being mostly finished, but sometimes the kid hadn't been in the mood to chill while daddy did his thing. Not that the baby was moving or anything yet—though it probably wouldn't be much longer—but he or she certainly contributed to Jazz's inability to stay up past ten p.m. most of the time.

Some rock star she was lately.

"Whatever. You're in the spotlight enough for people to want to get a piece of you." Harp forked up spicy chicken and veggies. Evidently her appetite hadn't deserted her like Jazz's had.

"I haven't been in contact with my sister in a decade. Molly was just a little thing back then. I just can't believe—"

"How old was she when you last saw her?"

"Six. That was more than ten years ago. She'll be...God, she'll be seventeen in a few days." Jazz fumbled for her guitar pick necklace, her link with Gray even when he wasn't around. Years ago he'd swapped the cheap chain the pick had originally been strung on for a sturdy silver one, which came in handy with how often she wrapped it around her fingers. "Maybe that's why she contacted me. It's a big birthday. You know, people get sentimental and stuff."

Harper didn't say anything. Jazz knew Harp was thinking that she was an idiot for giving Molly the benefit of the doubt. Harper was much more street-wise in some ways than Jazz was, in spite of the hell that was Jazz's teenage years. But God, was it so wrong to think that maybe someone had pure intentions? Not everyone was looking for a payday.

Your mama always was. And you know what they say about trees and branches...

"Look, I could've turned out money-hungry too, and I didn't," Jazz said, both to her friend and the voice in her head. It was a toss-up over which one was louder at the moment.

"Honey, you're one of the sweetest people I've ever known. I didn't even know people like you existed." Harp shook her head and broke a tortilla chip in half. "You befriend everyone and want to take care of the world. Considering your situation, it's amazing that you didn't become bitter. Instead you became the opposite."

"Oh, I've been bitter, believe me. But if I pushed people away, I knew I'd only end up even more alone."

"Did I mention self-aware too?" Harp grinned and dipped a chip in the bowl of freshly made salsa. "A lot of people twice your age haven't figured that one out yet. And as awesome as it is for you personality-wise, that trusting nature makes you a target. You can't afford to wear blinders about this situation, no matter who Molly is. I'm sorry that's the way things are, sweetie. I truly am."

"I'm not wearing blinders, and I'm not that trusting."

Yeah, okay, so she'd taken forever and a day to catch on to Gray being on coke. Actually, she hadn't caught on—Snake had told them all. But Gray was different. She'd always put him on a pedestal, and discovering that he wasn't perfect had taken her by surprise. It had also made her love him even more.

In her typical Harp way, her friend only dipped another chip rather than respond.

"How can you eat that?"

"Why? It's delish. Have some." Harp held out a chip dripping with salsa.

"No way." Jazz edged back in her chair and grabbed her belly. "I hurl the second tomatoes touch my lips." She waved a hand. "The smell's not much better."

"Oh. Sorry." Harp bit in with gusto, making Jazz laugh.

"Bitch. Better watch it or I'll break out that chocolate bar in my purse."

Harp grimaced. "Cruel and unusual punishment."

"Yeah, it's hard to have a good old-fashioned whine fest when our food choices are broken into two categories—puke and not-puke friendly."

Though truthfully, Jazz didn't mind at all. She *loved* being pregnant. Sure, she could've done without the nausea, exhaustion and swollen ankles, and the idea of squeezing out a small watermelon in front of a swarm of people in lab coats didn't turn her crank, but all the rest was awesome.

Including the fact that her boobs were now edging into D-cups, a fact Gray had no problem with whatsoever.

"The pregnancy thing does require some changing of our routines, yes. But at least we have someone to share it with."

"This is true. And our kids will be a couple months apart. We'll be able to put them in matching outfits and—"

"Even if you have a boy?" Harper grinned. "That should be interesting."

"Don't rub it in that your girl child success is assured." Jazz stuck out her tongue and went back to toying with her rice. "Gray's sure it's a girl."

"The big man was too. Me, I wasn't so sure. What do you think?"

"As long as it's healthy, I don't care." She really didn't. The fantasy of dressing a little girl up in pretty dresses and hair bows was just that. She'd be just as happy with a boy that looked like his handsome daddy.

"Yeah, because you'll keep having more until you get your girl."

"*Shh.* Don't give me ideas." Jazz grinned and pulled out her phone as it chimed with an incoming text. "Oh yay. Back to the studio. Just me today. I guess I didn't nail the intro of 'Torn to Pieces' or most of 'Monster.' And that's after about a hundred takes."

Harp loaded up another chip with salsa. "I don't know how you have the energy to keep whaling on those drums. Even heavy whisking taxes me some days."

"It's my job."

"Yeah, and you're incredible at it. If I ever decide to go for mushroom on my pizza instead of sausage, I'm totally demanding that you deliver."

Jazz choked on her bite of rice and grabbed her iced tea to wash it down while she sputtered out a laugh. This was what best friends were for. Making you grin no matter how lousy you felt. Even when you technically had no reason to feel lousy, because you were happier than you'd ever been in your life.

"There, that's better. I need my Jazz smiling or else I'll go back to work all bitchy. And I already have budget overruns on the costs for that Jamison job and..."

Jazz tuned Harper out while she went back to picking at her lunch. She didn't mean to, but she desperately needed a nap. Gray hadn't come home until super late last night thanks to some new alt rockers he was working with, and as usual, Jazz hadn't been able to sleep without him beside her. Her inability to sleep alone was stupid, considering she'd gone to bed by herself until recently without any ill effects. She and Gray had only been together a short time, not counting the almost decade of extended mental foreplay beforehand. But that didn't change the sigh of relief she breathed every time he slipped under the covers with her and slid his arm around her to tug her close.

"Oh crap. Annie's got the flu and she's gotta go home early." Harper was already rising and shoving her cell phone into her purse. "I hate to eat and run but we have all those stupid canapés to finish."

Jazz smothered a sigh. "Sure, of course." She'd lost the thread of the conversation and now she was going to have to finish her lunch alone. She pushed her plate away. Not that she was hungry anyway. "I'm sorry Annie's sick. Can I help? I could fill in—"

"We're also making meatballs this afternoon, which means big vats of spicy red sauce."

Jazz shuddered. "Never mind. Good luck."

Harper laughed and patted Jazz's shoulder. "Keep me posted on the Molly situation, okay? And talk to Gray. You know you won't get straightened out until you do."

Jazz lifted her chin. "I'm an independent career woman. I don't need to check in with my significant other every five minutes."

Harper nodded soberly. "Of course not. Do it anyway. For me. And finish your lunch. You're already the size of a string bean."

"Yes, Mom."

"Pot, kettle," Harper said in a singsong voice, backing up with a wave.

"Uh-huh. Send Annie my love. I'll talk to you later."

Jazz's smile lasted until the door swung closed behind her friend. Then she huffed out a breath and viewed her mostly full plate like a climber standing at the bottom of Mount Everest. This lack of an appetite thing sucked.

As did being too unnerved to open a damn envelope.

She picked it up again, flipping it over a few times. She could do this. Whatever it said didn't really matter. She had her own budding family now, both with Gray and with the band of misfits she loved so much. As much as she still missed her baby sister, this couldn't hurt her if she didn't let it.

Van Morrison's "Brown-Eyed Girl" began playing in her purse, Gray's ringtone, and she flushed as she always did. God, that song. Gray had once modified it to fit her blue eyes and it never failed to make her smile.

She dropped the envelope like her fingers had been singed in favor of digging out her cell. "Hello," she said, her voice coming out breathier than she intended.

"Well, hello to you too."

She grinned at his deep, honeyed tone. Gray's rasp did crazy things to her belly when he wasn't trying. When he put any effort into it, he slayed her dead. "Wow, only one o'clock and I get the sex voice? To what do I owe this honor?"

"You answered the phone sounding sexy, so I felt like I should respond in kind. And to carry on the theme, what're you wearing?"

"Right now?" She glanced down at her bright pink V-necked top—and the clump of pork sitting on her left boob. "I'm wearing part of Fiesta Cantina's number six special. The rest is still on my plate."

His rich laughter didn't last long. "Why aren't you packing it away?"

Her fingers started to creep across the scarred tabletop to the envelope again before she mentally slapped them back. "I'm not that hungry."

Wrong answer.

"Why not? Are you feeling okay?"

"Sure. You know, I don't have to eat twenty-four/seven. I'm allowed to take breaks."

"If you're not eating, something's wrong. Are you sure you're not sick? Is it the morning sickness again? I thought you were better. What about those pills? They're supposed to help. Or crackers. Deak said that—"

"Take a breath," she advised. "And sweetie, as much as I appreciate the barrage of advice, once you bring another non-child-bearing, penis-toting individual into the conversation, the pregnancy help is over."

"He's going to be a father," he said, clearly affronted, which only made her grin.

"Yes, he is. And he still has a penis. From what I've heard, it's really freaking hu—"

"Stop this train, I'm getting off."

She couldn't help giggling. "Sorry. Girl talk. You know how it is. I promise, I told Harper you're built like a cross between a stallion and a gorilla, with some throwback tendencies to a T-Rex."

"You seriously talk to Harper about my dick? Never mind. I don't want to know."

"I only say flattering things."

"Great. Now I'm the one who wants to throw up."

She giggled again, knowing he was just kidding and not the least bit bothered. Gray didn't have anything to worry about in the meat-packing department, and he damn well knew it. "So what's up? I don't suppose you can join me for a late lunch? Harp had to leave."

"Aww, babe, I can't. I wish I could."

"That's okay." Her smile drooped under the weight of her newly squashed hopes. "I'll see you later."

"That's why I'm calling. I'm going to be late tonight. That band I'm working with, The Grunge? They want me to head over to their practice space in Ventura. Something about getting their vibe. No fucking clue what that means, but I'm going because I think these guys are on the way up. Do you know what that could mean for us if their album breaks in a major way?"

She bit her lip and tucked the offending envelope under her napkin, out of sight. "If *our* album breaks in a major way, why do we need to worry about theirs?"

His sigh wasn't unexpected, but that didn't mean it didn't hurt just the same. "Babe, we've been over this. We can't just count on Oblivion when we have a kid on the way. We have to be responsible enough to—"

"Wait, hold up. I'm not being responsible? I'm about to head back into the studio to do another half dozen takes on my parts of the songs you've already finished when I have an unending need to pee and can't decide if I'm full, I'm hungry or if I'm going to puke."

"Why do you have to go back into the studio? You're always flawless."

That had been sticking in her craw too, though she hadn't fully acknowledged it since the Molly situation had taken top billing. She wasn't used to not getting it right the first time. The rest of her life, hell yes. She was usually a moving fail from one day to the next. But her music normally came through for her.

"Apparently not now, I'm not." She rubbed her eyes and tried to dial back the bitchy in her tone. He didn't deserve it. He was just trying to take care of them. "I'm just cranky and hot and want to curl up somewhere to sleep. Don't mind me."

"Call the studio and tell them to book you later in the week instead if you aren't feeling well."

"Does that mean you'll come to bed with me and keep me company?"

His silence ate away at the hint of amusement that tried creeping back. She knew he couldn't come home. He'd just said as much, and what was keeping him away would benefit both of them. So why did she keep pushing him?

Because you need to talk to him about Molly, and you can't say the damn words.

"I wish I could. If you need me, just call."

"When you're stuck in Ventura? Fat lot of good that'll do me." As soon as the words were out, she wanted to snatch them back, but she couldn't.

God, she needed to stuff a handful of tortilla chips in her mouth unless she wanted to end up divorced before they'd even gotten married.

"Jesus, Jazz, this is for our future. And our child's future. You get that, right? I'm trying to make certain we have a solid base."

"I understand all of that. That base is part of why I'm about to go do my job. Have a good day." She clicked off and set down the phone, cursing herself under her breath. She hadn't said *I love you*, and the last time she'd done that, he'd gotten beaten up and nearly killed. It was bad juju, and she was being a bitch to him for absolutely no reason.

Well, other than the fact that she hated having to share him with anyone after all the years they'd spent in denial about their feelings. That wasn't fair to him. Besides, they were going to have a lifetime together.

She should call him back and apologize.

Grabbing her phone, she pressed the number one speed dial, already anticipating hearing his husky, deep voice. She was so in love with him that it made her stupid. Surely that erased some of her bitch points, right? She'd even take the hormonal pregnancy discount if it eased some of this damn guilt.

Guilt that only compounded when the call went straight to voicemail.

She hung up without saying anything, feeling utterly miserable. He never avoided her calls. And she never wimped out on apologizing when it was due.

Swallowing hard, she tossed her phone in her purse and dug out her wallet. The waiter had dropped off the bill when she was on the phone with Gray, and the total was more than the bills she had in her wallet. Harper had forgotten to chip in her share in her hurry to leave.

Jazz sighed and dug out the ATM card she saved for emergencies. Growing up as a foster kid had made her pretty frugal, and being in a semi-famous band hadn't changed that. Yet another reason why Gray's lectures about responsibility rubbed her raw. She'd always been responsible about money. She'd even bailed *him* out when—

No. She blew out a breath. Not going there. She'd spent enough time on Snarky Street for one afternoon.

She paid the bill and checked her silent phone one more fruitless time before heading down to Ripper Records' in-house studio. Six hours plus later, her sections were finished—again— and she was free to leave.

Good thing because she was falling asleep on her feet.

Oblivion's manager Lila walked her out to her car, her sharp heels clicking on the pavement. "So are you okay to drive home?"

Jazz cut her a glance. "Why wouldn't I be?"

"Because you're so pale I could see my reflection in your cheek." Lila gripped Jazz's arm and tapped her wrist. "Pulse is strong. Are you feeling faint?"

Jazz had to laugh. She'd never been mothered so much in her life as she had been since becoming pregnant. As soon as she had the thought, the laughter died.

She'd never been really mothered, not the right way. Even as a child, she hadn't been her mother's first priority. Or even fifth. So no wonder it felt so strange—and wonderful—to have people she cared about fussing over her at every turn.

Gray would fuss over her when he got home, she just knew it. He hadn't called all day because he was working, not because he thought she was an obnoxious, ungrateful wench.

Or something even worse.

"I'm fine, I promise. I'm just a little tired. It was a long day."

"It was, but you nailed your parts. I think this album is finally almost in the can, minus a bit more finessing. Did I mention we're bringing Margo back in too? Her section needed some work as well." Lila shook her head. "So odd. You two are the biggest perfectionists yet you both needed more studio time." Almost as an afterthought, she glanced at Jazz's belly with an expression akin to trepidation. "Though I suppose in your case the implant had something to do with that."

"The implant?" Jazz snorted out a laugh as she pried her car keys out of her purse. Surreptitiously, she checked her silent phone one more time. Maybe it wasn't working. Perhaps she should borrow Lila's. She glanced up to see her friend peering down at her with a knowing gleam in her eyes.

So much for surreptitious.

"Missing your man, hmm?"

"No," Jazz said, a little too quickly. "Just keeping an eye on...things."

"Mmm-hmm. Things like where he is and where he's sticking it."

Surely she'd misheard her. "Say what?"

Lila slid a hand over her hair, smoothing the pin-straight strands into place. Not that they'd been out of place to begin with. "Nothing. That's just my own insecurities talking. Gray would never do that to you while you were pregnant."

"But he would some other time?" Jazz couldn't keep the sharpness from her tone. "Li, what are you getting at?"

Lila surprised Jazz by leaning against the side of the used car Gray had bought earlier that month. Now that they were building their family, he'd wanted her to have something reliable and not to have to rely on the kindness of friends or the band truck for transportation.

Still though, it was a beat-up vehicle with its share of LA dirt smudged on the paint, which wouldn't go well with Lila's pristine pale pink suit.

"I'm not getting at anything except I'm more than a little bitter and a lot jealous."

"Of what? Of who?"

Lila smiled. "You, silly. Look at you. You're glowing."

"A minute ago you said I was Casper's twin."

"Okay, so today the light's weaker than some days, but still." Lila grabbed Jazz's hands and held them out to the sides. "You're absolutely gorgeous. Soon you're going to be walking around with a big belly, and he loves you just that way. That's rather incredible."

Jazz frowned. If today had taught her anything, it was to not read more into what was said than the actual words. She would employ that same newfound wisdom when and if she womaned up enough to read Molly's letter sometime this century.

Right now she would use her new skills to respond more proactively to Lila's statement.

"Did someone tell you they didn't like the way a woman looked when she was pregnant?" she asked softly.

That was one thing she would never have to worry about with Gray. If anything, he found her even more desirable now. He had his hands all over her constantly and told her all the time that he couldn't wait to see her body change.

Lila lowered her gaze to the ground. "Is it that obvious?"

"No. Eight hours ago, I would've assumed you were trying to say I looked fat and it was a miracle that Gray still thought I was attractive. This morning, I ate Bitchy Bran Flakes for breakfast and was ready to bite people's heads off. I've had an attitude shift since then."

Lila smiled. "Let me guess. It involved a lunchtime quickie before you got here."

"I wish." Jazz sagged against the car. Screw the dust. "We haven't had sex in three days."

"Oh, the horrors." Lila examined her manicure, hesitating before she continued speaking. "Do you know how long it's been since I've had sex?"

Lila never talked about her personal life. Ever. Even the word *sex* falling out of her pale pink lips seemed impossibly crude. "Uh—"

"More than six years."

"Oh. Wow. Um. Wow."

Lila surprised her by laughing. "Yes, wow. Yet I manage to function just the same."

"So I shouldn't whine about three days, I guess. Sorry. I didn't realize. Are you just...really particular or—"

"More that I don't feel it's proper to compromise my vows. Marriage vows," she added when Jazz stared.

"You're married? Why the hell aren't you having sex then?" Jazz clapped a hand over her mouth. "Sorry. Uncalled for. Not my business. But seriously, why? That's like having Nutella in the cupboard and only eating plain crackers."

Lila laughed, shaking her head. "My husband has not ever been and will never be considered Nutella. He's more of a dry fruit spread with too many seeds."

"Okay," Jazz said slowly. It really wasn't her business. She had no reason to ask. "But don't you, you know, get horny?"

"Of course. But I don't need a man for that." Lila eased off the car and stood bow-straight as she cast a critical look at Jazz. "Go home and get some rest. I want you to have some pink in your cheeks the next time I see you." Lila leaned in and shocked the hell out of her by giving her a brief, semi-awkward hug then stepped back. "Eat too. Something light that won't upset the baby this late. Good work today," she called, starting back toward the studio at a blistering clip.

She was gone before Jazz found her voice.

Shaking her head, Jazz unlocked the car and slipped inside. Her stomach rumbled. It was now creeping toward eight o'clock.

A greasy meal would hit the spot. Maybe a double cheeseburger with an extra side of pickles or—

Eat too. Something light that won't upset the baby this late.

Jazz turned the key in the ignition. For someone who wasn't a mom, Lila sure had a mom-like way about her. And she was right. The baby probably wouldn't mind—or even know—if she shoved a pile of fast food down her throat, but she would. She had to think *responsibly.*

Fuck that word.

She ended up taking a detour to the grocery store. She loaded up her cart with some staples, since Simon had taken to popping her candy-like vitamins and drinking her whole milk. When she started breastfeeding, she was tempted to dump some in the carton and not tell him. It would only serve him right.

He'd probably happily drink it anyway, the freak.

She gave in to a pack of chocolate chip cookies and to checking her phone twice, though she compensated by adding extra vegetables to her cart. Vegetables were a suitable penance for everything. And for good measure, she'd go for her recommended daily thirty minute walk when she arrived home. Unless Gray was there, of course. Then she'd apologize profusely, ask him about his day like a good little almost-wifey then jump the holy hell out of him.

She shuddered, thinking of Lila as she loaded her groceries into the trunk. Six years with no sex seemed like cruel and unusual punishment. She'd had some serious dry spells of her own, often lasting a year or more, but she'd balanced that scale by boinking like bunnies with Gray since they'd gotten together. Then there was that one threesome she'd had in days of yore...

Yeah, not going there. Thank God that particular bone had been tucked into its proper closet, never to be unearthed again. She hoped.

In under an hour, she arrived home and put away her groceries, kicked Simon's feet off the coffee table just to piss in his Cheerios, exchanged some snark with Nick and enjoyed a big bear hug from Deacon. Harper was out doing her catering thing, and though Jazz missed her, it was probably just as well. Harper and Deak would be moving out as soon as their new house was ready and she had to get used to not having her best friend under the same roof.

Her best friend that wasn't Gray, that is. He would always come first in everything with her, as he had since the day she'd moved into his parents' house at the age of fourteen. She still remembered the way he'd swaggered into the living room that first day, wearing a vintage Dokken T-shirt and a face full of attitude. Then he'd noticed the guitar in her lap and the most beautiful friendship of her life had been born.

Glancing down, she rubbed her belly and tried to stem the tide of emotions that seemed way too close to the surface lately. She wanted to blame her hormones. Hell, she'd blame the phases of the moon if she could. Anything was better than realizing that with every passing day of her pregnancy, her family was creeping back into her thoughts. *Her* family, not Gray's, though she missed them too in spite of everything that had happened between them. Her mama.

And Molly.

Bringing a new life into the world was something to share with those you were close to. She hadn't been close to her birth family in too many years to count but that didn't mean she didn't miss them. It didn't mean she didn't hope way down deep that maybe someday they could be reunited.

"Stupid, foolish romantic heart," she said under her breath. She hurried into the bathroom and shed her clothes before she could be tempted to dig out Molly's letter again. She would open it when she was ready.

She would be soon. Maybe. Possibly.

She carried her bath stuff to the tub, then added a bunch of bubbles before slipping into the water. The surprisingly cool spring day had make her fantasize about a hot soak all evening. Naturally she'd wished Gray would be home to join her, but as that wasn't in the cards, she was going to have a fine time on her own.

After sighing her way through the first few steamy minutes, she fumbled for the expensive pair of waterproof headphones she'd bought for this very purpose. She turned on her waterproof radio, setting it to the classical channel before shifting around so her belly poked through the bubbles.

"You ready for the nightly concert, kiddo? Sorry about the noise earlier. Mommy screwed up her part so she had to keep doing it over and over. I bet you probably hate 'Monster' now. Me too, but it'll be kickass live. Uh, I mean kickbutt." She cast a glance skyward and sent up a quick apology. Lord, this parenting thing wasn't easy, and she hadn't even gone through childbirth yet. "Anyway, this music is much more suitable for bedtime. If it doesn't put you to sleep, I don't know what will."

Carefully, she placed the padded headphones on either side of her slightly rounded belly and turned up the volume until she could just barely hear the strains of Chopin. Supposedly babies who were exposed to classical music in the womb were much more likely to be prodigies. She didn't care if her child was a prodigy. All she wanted was for him or her to be smart and happy and know how much he or she was loved. So very loved.

If the kid happened to be born loving music, that would be a plus.

She tipped her head backward against her little inflatable bath pillow and closed her eyes. God, she was so tired. Exhausted. Worrying all day about the Molly thing and then the stupid not-quite-an-argument with Gray and his subsequent radio silence had worn her down. She knew he was probably just working. He'd told her he was, and she believed him.

She'd believed him before too.

Goose bumps flared over her pinkening skin and she rubbed them away, unwilling to go down that path. He'd kicked the drugs. He'd gotten treatment and he was committed to his sobriety. Borrowing trouble never did anyone any favors.

Maybe if she slept for a bit, when she woke up, Gray would be there.

But what if he wasn't?

CHAPTER TWO

Gray walked into the bedroom he shared with Jazz at Oblivion's rented house in the Hollywood Hills, his head buzzing with chords and lyrics. That was his favorite part about all-day and night sessions. If he kept at it, eventually the music hijacked his consciousness and everyday life became superfluous. Problems faded away. Paying bills and forgetting to pick up a card for a birthday or to drop off the dry cleaning—ha, as if the band got stuff dry cleaned—all ceased to be important.

Luckily he'd found that was still true for him even when he wasn't creating the music on his guitar, but with his pen. In the short time he'd been farming out his songs to artists, he'd already begun to note differences. Some didn't want what he was selling and intended to fight him at every turn. Others wanted to make sure he knew they needed to put their own mark on his lyrics. Some said it confrontationally, as if they expected him to be a diva about the whole process.

He truly didn't give a shit. He understood a band needing to add their own flair to the lyrics he came up with. Actually he preferred that. He didn't want his songs sung by robots just collecting a paycheck. Music *mattered*.

When the group he worked with was like today's band, The Grunge, collaboration became seriously fun. They'd let him into their practice space and treated him like one of them, rather than an unwanted emissary sent over by a hostile record company as some groups tended to do. By the end of the night, they'd worked on two solid songs and were halfway to a third. He'd even gotten to jam with them, because they were Oblivion fans. How cool was that?

He started to call out for Jazz, then noticed the bathroom door was cracked open and light beamed out from underneath. He grinned and shucked his T-shirt, ready to make up for their sort of argument earlier. He'd been driving without his hands-free headset when her second call had come through, and though he'd fumbled for the phone anyway, he hadn't gotten it in time. As tempted as he'd been to call her back, he'd known that they would probably get into it again and he needed to keep his head in the game.

Somehow he had to figure out how to express to her the importance of him logging some serious songwriting credentials. If he could crack that nut, they wouldn't have to worry financially for a damn long time, but she didn't seem to understand that. So he would keep trying.

In the meantime, he'd make it up to her for their fight the best way he knew how.

His hand lowered to the button of his jeans as he licked his lips and walked toward the partially open door. He could already tell she'd used that watermelon body wash again, and the scent instantly made him hard. Nudging the door open with his foot, he leaned inside, ready to drop his jeans and boxers in about five seconds flat if she seemed interested.

Instead he froze, the greeting on his lips turning into a long exhale.

She was asleep in the tub. The frothy water lapping around her belly and breasts didn't hide the headphones on her stomach. Tinny classical music played while she slept. Her cheeks were rosy from the heat, her lashes heavy and dark on her porcelain skin. The warmth had pinkened her up, increasing the flush on her throat and nipples.

He shifted. Fuck, he shouldn't look at her nipples right now. Not when he had a goddamn lump in his throat from the simple sight of her with those headphones, cradling their baby. She'd mentioned playing music for the baby but he'd never actually *seen* it. He had no choice but to drop to his knees beside the tub to rouse her with soft fingertips on her damp cheek.

"Hey," he murmured when her lids lifted drowsily. "I'm sorry to wake you." He slipped his hand into the water and frowned at how cool it was. "Come on, let's get you dried off and into bed."

"Nuh-uh." She sat up and nudged away his hand. "I'm fine. What time is it?" Then she slumped back down, sending the headphones plopping into the water. "You're here."

"Of course I'm here." He fished out her headphones and shook them off. "Not sure *these* will be here for much longer though."

"They're waterproof. I paid a mint for them so the baby could listen to music while I napped." She yawned. "Turns out napping is something I want to do a lot lately."

He frowned, noticing the paleness of her cheeks now that the warm water flush was fading. "You're working yourself too hard. Did you finish in the studio?"

"Yeah." She turned her cheek toward her inflatable pillow, her eyes already closing again. "Now give me my headphones and I'll just doze a little longer."

"Nope. You're headed to bed. Non-negotiable."

"But—"

"Non-negotiable," he repeated, setting the headphones aside before rising and lifting her out of the tub in spite of her sputtering. Foamy water splashed everywhere, dripping from her body as he carted her into the bedroom and laid her down on their bed. "Stay," he said when she leaned up on one elbow.

"I'm not a damn dog."

"No. But you're incredibly beautiful and I want to towel down my wife. Is that okay?"

Watching her face soften eased the irritation flaring to life inside of him. He wanted to put her in a bubble and keep her and the baby safe from all threats, whether they were financial difficulties or cold bathwater. Was that so wrong? Wasn't that his *job*?

"I'm not your wife yet," she said quietly. "Not technically."

He headed into the bathroom to grab a thick purple towel and returned to sit beside her on the bed. He lifted her arm and began to dry her, slowly and methodically. Not leaving a solitary spot on her arm untouched until she let out a laugh. "What is this? Death by terrycloth?"

He didn't smile. Nor did he stop drying her off. He moved down to her hip, studying it intently to avoid gazing at the rosy pink slit between her legs. "I'm going to be overbearing with you, and you're just going to have to deal with it, Edwards. I know you're a strong woman. You'd have to be to put up with my stupid ass. But when it's you and me and we're alone, I need to take care of you. It's this...*urge* inside me."

"Is that so?"

The amusement in her tone made him turn his head. Her annoyance had disappeared as fast as it had come, leaving her smiling and gorgeous and *damp*. Suddenly, not discovering if she was wet all over seemed like a terrible waste. "It's so," he said, moving forward to catch her laughter with his mouth.

"I'm not supposed to complain about this." Easing back, she tilted her head, one dark curl slipping into her eyes. "I'm supposed to just lie here and take it."

Taking her statement for the invitation it was, he tossed aside the towel and shifted on top of her, careful to lift his torso off hers as they settled into the pillows. As usual, she realized what he was doing and grabbed his ass, pulling him down on top of her hard enough that his lips crushed onto hers. He gripped her hair in both hands, losing himself in the sensation of her tongue sliding sensuously over his. Tangling, teasing. His breathing hitched when she wrapped her leg around his hip and arched against him, rubbing her bare pussy over the rigid length trapped unforgivingly in his jeans. "Missed you today," she whispered, biting his lower lip. "Don't want to ever fight again."

"I do." He saw the hurt flash into her drowsy gaze before he grinned and licked a path down her throat. "Because I sure as hell have no problem with the makeup sex."

"Jerk." She laughed and smacked his shoulder before wiggling out from under his body. She sat up and grabbed the towel, briskly drying her hair.

"Jeez, shut me down, why don't you?" Without bothering to hide it, he adjusted himself. Touching his cock through the denim added a new layer of torture. "I never realized you were into punishment, Mistress Jasmine."

Her lips barely twitched. "I'm not. We just need to talk."

"That sounds ominous. Are you leaving me for a Nordic ski instructor named Sven?"

"You know I can't ski. Besides, I have this thing for emo rockers." She gave him a flirty smile over one shoulder that didn't quite reach her eyes and rose to her feet when he made a grab for her. "I need you to see something. Then you'll understand why I was so out of sorts today."

"I've already seen plenty, and now you're walking away. Christ." He flopped down on the mattress and indulged in an extended moment of masochism by watching her cross the room to the dresser.

Her body had started out as a damn work of art, and now that her curves were becoming fuller, she was even hotter. That tiny baby bump was going to do him in. He was probably developing a fetish.

Damn, he wanted to kiss and lick every square inch of her, then do it all over again.

"An envelope?" he asked as she turned back.

Saying nothing, she rejoined him on the bed and handed it to him. The name in the corner didn't register at first. When it did, he glanced at her in surprise. "Your sister?"

She nodded, her eyes too bright.

He turned the envelope over, intending to pull out the contents, only to see it was still sealed. He flipped it over again. "Why haven't you opened it?"

"Because I can't." She pulled her knees up to her chest and rested her chin on them, and for a second, he was thrown back into the past. *Their* past, when she used to come into his bedroom at his parents' house and they'd talk and laugh and play their guitars for hours. She looked just as young and innocent now as she had all those years ago, though she'd lived through more difficult shit than he would wish on his worst enemy. But it hadn't hardened her. Somehow the beautiful streak of vulnerability he'd noticed the day they'd met still shone through her blue eyes and made his hands ball into fists against any unseen threat.

She was his, and he would protect her no matter the cost.

"Why?" He forced his voice to remain level. "Has she contacted you before?"

"No. This was the first time. But I needed to talk about it with you." She lowered her head until the long hanks of her wet hair fell down over her cheek. "Maybe that makes me weak or foolish or sappy, but I needed you to tell me it would be okay no matter what. That if she wants to see me, it's going to be fine. That if she never wants to see me, it's not going to break me any more than I've already been broke."

"And I blew you off," he said, clenching his fist around the envelope for an all new reason. The thin paper wrinkled, and he smoothed it with his thumb.

"No, you didn't. You were working and I was being a selfish brat. I've spent so many years without you that I guess part of me doesn't believe this is real. That you're really here and you really love me. That this baby is going to arrive and he or she is going to be whole and perfect and hopefully will pick the drums over the guitar, because he or she has true taste." Her mouth quirked up on the last bit, but she still didn't look at him. "This letter—it felt like the beginning of our end," she whispered. "Here's the other shoe. Now watch it drop."

"Jazz, look at me." When she didn't, he cupped his hand under her jaw and lifted her head until they were eye-to-eye. "This isn't our end. We don't have one. We might have had the longest beginning in the history of life, but now we're on the road to our future. No detours. No back alleys. No fucking shoes."

"Why is she contacting me now? It's been so long."

"I have some ideas," he said, wishing he could snatch back the words when she closed her eyes.

"You think she wants all the money I don't have," she said, sounding utterly exhausted. "Harper thought the same."

"You talked about this with Harper first?"

"She was available," she said, twisting the knife and leaving him to bleed.

He moved back and set the envelope on the mattress between them, hating its presence almost as much as he hated this endless loop they'd gotten caught on since this afternoon. Had they been overdue? Things had been going so well. In the weeks since he'd been back from rehab, they hadn't fought once. All they'd done was talk, and laugh, and make love. And yes, there were times when he caught her looking at him too long and hard, as if she were waiting for minute cracks to form in his armor. Once an addict, always an addict some said, and he wasn't naïve enough to think she never wondered if he'd fall off the wagon.

But that was one concern in the middle of a hell of a lot of happiness. They were finally building their lives together, and nothing else could intrude on their bubble of bliss.

Until this. And the work that had unintentionally taken him away from her when she needed him most.

"You should've told me," he said, buttoning his jeans. "I can't read your mind."

He expected her to argue. Not to say softly, "I know. I'm sorry."

"Me too." He heaved out a breath and wrapped his arm around her, tugging her against his chest where she belonged. "I'm sorry I wasn't there, baby."

"It's not your fault. You were just taking care. You know, because of that *urge* you have." Her lips curved but it didn't take a genius to see her heart wasn't in it. She toyed with the button on his jeans, flipping it open again and nearly making him groan. "I have urges too."

"Yeah, and yours aren't helping mine when you're sitting around naked and I have the hard-on from hell."

Her giggle acted as a balm to his soul. He'd cheerfully kill to hear that sound every hour of every day for the rest of his life.

"You know, there's one way we could stop debating what Molly wants," he said, brushing a kiss over the top of her head. She smelled like soap and watermelon, as fresh and pure as a summer's day.

Nodding, she picked up the envelope and pushed it at his chest. "You open it."

"Is this a variation on how you open your Christmas gifts as if someone is giving you a poisonous snake rather than a good surprise?"

"Yes. Open it for me. Please."

With one glance into those big, pleading eyes, he was sunk, and they both knew it. He slid his finger under the flap of the envelope and tugged out the single sheet of lined notebook paper, reading the words written in fat, loopy swirls as dispassionately as a trial judge presiding in court.

Jazz nudged his arm. "Well?"

He refolded the paper and slid it back in the envelope. Amazing how within a few moments, plans could begin to take shape in your mind, and then swiftly become so solidified that there seemed to be no other option. None you wanted to take anyway.

"She wants to meet with you. Us," he clarified, because there would never be anything but an *us* in reference to either of them ever again. They were a team that had been benched for too long. "She's heard good things about the band. Thinks we're kickass."

Jazz winced and cupped her hand over her belly. "Shh."

He had to laugh. He swore all the time, from *fuck* to *damn* to *shit* and everything in between. But it was *kickass* that stirred her fledgling mothering instincts.

"God, I love you." Her head came up and he could tell by her expression that he'd taken her by surprise. Good. He needed to do that more often. She needed to learn that not all boxes with pretty bows contained hissing, snapping creatures inside.

She deserved to be spoiled, *treasured*, and he intended to start now.

"Even though I'm occasionally witchy and try to give you a hard time for just being a decent guy?" She screwed up her mouth and toyed with the button on his jeans. "I get the money thing, I do, but I gotta say, it doesn't matter to me."

"Duly noted," he said drily, stilling her hand before his cock did something unseemly like bust right through his zipper.

"I know we need money, especially if we're going to buy a house—"

"There is no *if*. We're having a baby. We can't live here with these slobs forever."

She lifted a brow at the piles of his clothes strewn around the room, along with sneakers, notebooks and assorted other crap. "Pot? Your kettle is calling."

"Hey. You're supposed to overlook my flaws." He slipped his hand into her hair and turned her mouth toward his, brushing a soft kiss over her lips.

"I do. I try to." She edged back and he smothered a groan as she gave him a serious look that proved any chances for sex were on a speed boat heading in the opposite direction. "There's something else I have to tell you."

"More revelations." He took her hand and placed it on his chest, right over his heart. "Hit me."

"When you didn't call me back and the day wore on without hearing from you, a small part of me wondered if..." She trailed off, but he didn't need to hear the rest.

"You wondered if I'd fallen into a baggie of blow."

She lowered her head. "I'm sorry. I didn't really think it, deep down. I guess I still just worry too much."

"You're entitled. After what we went through, who can blame you? And yes, it was *we*. I was the one with the problem, but I dragged you down with me. And if you hadn't been there, it's entirely possible I'd still be in the same place."

Her minty exhale puffed against his cheek. "You're not mad?"

"No." He tucked her hair behind her ears with gentle fingers. "I don't blame you one bit for thinking that. It hasn't been that long."

"I know, but I'm supposed to believe in you. And I do, I swear, I just—" She shut her eyes, shaking her head. "I just keep wondering when I'm going to wake up and this is all going to go away."

"Never. You're awake, and it's only going to get better from here."

Her slow smile teased out her rarely seen dimples. "Not. Possible."

We'll see about that.

"Don't feel guilty for feeling what anyone would. Besides, all it does is provide me with more motivation to become the man you always believed I was."

"That's who you are already."

"Getting there." He nuzzled her neck, lapping at the beads of water still clinging to her skin. So many spots he hadn't come close to drying yet. And others he hadn't begun to get wet enough. "Even if you want me to hang out here all day, singing dirty songs to you while I lick your—"

"Gray!" Her screech ended on a laugh as she covered her belly. "The baby can hear you."

"Hmm. The baby's about to hear and feel something much more dirty than what I just said. A live re-enactment, let's say." She grinned, but he didn't miss how her gaze shifted to the envelope he'd set next to his hip. Sighing, he pulled out the paper and held it out to her. "You know you won't be able to relax until you read it. Which is kind of a hit to my skills of sexual persuasion, but whatever."

She snatched the paper and read it quickly, tugging her lower lip between her teeth while he shifted restlessly and cursed his jeans. He was never wearing denim again. Better, he was never wearing denim again and she needed to start wearing something shapeless like muu muus. That was the only way he could concentrate on not wanting to jump her. *Especially* now that she was pregnant.

"She's living in San Jose."

"Yeah."

"That's near San Fran."

"Since we're doing geography lessons," he leaned forward and kissed her bare shoulder, "can I map out some new territory?"

"It's not new. You've mapped all of my territories many times." She gave him a distracted smile and went back to the letter. "She doesn't mention mom."

"No. She doesn't."

"Why do you think that is?"

"Maybe your mom dumped her in the system when she didn't want to deal with her anymore too." He swore under his breath at the horrified glance she shot him. "I'm sure that didn't happen."

"It could have. What if she's on her own? What if she's been dealing with the same shit I went through, except she's all alone?"

She scrambled off the bed and crossed to the dresser to tug out a nearly sheer pink nightie. She pulled it over her head and pushed a hand through her hair, only messing it up more. "Why didn't she contact me before now?"

"She could be just a normal teenager, living in a crappy apartment and hating her mom like a lot of teenagers do. That could be why she didn't mention her."

She spun to face him. "You don't really think that."

He rose to walk over to her, hating the tension radiating off her in waves. Yes, he worried too much, but Christ, he didn't want her to be agitated when she was already so exhausted. It wasn't good for her or the baby.

"Don't," she said before he could speak. "I'm not some fragile flower that's going to fall apart if you blow on me too hard. I'm perfectly healthy. This baby is perfectly healthy. I have every right to be concerned about my sister." She turned toward him and pressed her fist against his pec. "To be fucking pissed," she said in an undertone that he knew was for the baby's sake.

Unlike her own mother, Jazz never forgot her own child for a second.

"I know you're both healthy. I also know that you need to get some sleep."

"That's not why you want me in that bed," she said, punching his chest.

He winced. His woman had strong as hell hands. "Pleading the fifth." Her exasperated sigh made him tip her face up to his. "What do you want to do? Tell me, and we'll make it happen."

She didn't hesitate. "I want to go to the address she listed as soon as possible."

He nodded. "Already on it." The moment he'd read that San Jose address written in swooping purple ink, a plan had begun to form in his mind. One so perfect he wondered how he hadn't thought of it before.

They'd been too busy, probably. Since he left rehab, everything had been non-stop. Between making up what he'd missed in the studio for the new album, and assimilating into regular life again as a sober person, not to mention finding out he was going to be a father—yeah, there hadn't been a lot of time to get his romance on. Much to his regret.

Because if anyone deserved a lifetime of romance, it was the woman standing before him, her gaze pinpointed somewhere in the distance.

With her sister. Already.

"I have to head back to Ventura tomorrow. We're in the middle of a song, and they want to nail down one more for the album, but then...what?" he asked as her shoulders drooped. "What's wrong?"

"Don't you remember what tomorrow is?"

He searched his brain then turned toward the dresser where he'd dumped his phone. "Shit. I forgot."

"You forgot when we're going to find out our baby's sex?"

He didn't have to look back at her to hear the tears in her voice. His already frayed nerves thinned just a bit more. "Yeah, well, I'm failing all over the place today. I would've remembered."

"When? After we missed the appointment?"

"Jesus, Jazz. Cut me some slack. You're hauling the kid around. You can't forget stuff like that."

"You shouldn't forget either. It's half yours. Or maybe you don't care. Maybe it doesn't matter."

He braced his hands on the edge of the dresser and prayed for strength. Times like this, he really missed being able to drink, though he'd never had much of a taste for the stuff. "You're right," he said, turning back. "It absolutely does not matter."

Tears hovered in her huge eyes and made his gut clench. "How can you say that?"

"Because I don't care if it's a boy or a girl or a mini Martian. It's ours and it's perfect and I'm going to love it regardless."

Her chin wobbled. "I hate when you're so sweet that I feel like a horrible wretch."

He laughed and drew her into the circle of his arms. "You should. Thinking I don't care? C'mon now. Have I or have I not worshipped your belly every moment since you told me you were pregnant?"

"You have, but I kind of thought that was like a fetish."

"So?"

She hiccupped out a laugh. "Sorry. I've turned into Pregzilla."

"No, you haven't, honey," he said in the most patronizing voice possible, causing her to laugh harder as she shoved him back.

"Who're you calling?" She inclined her chin at the phone he still gripped.

"The band I worked with today."

"This late?"

His eyebrow winged up. "You really have turned into Pregzilla. What music guys do you know who sleep before midnight?"

"Guys *and* girls. Sexist jerk." But she grinned as she thumped him in the gut.

Shaking his head, he called Luc, the lead singer of The Grunge. After a quick greeting, he got right to the point. "Look, tomorrow's jam session isn't going to work. I have an appointment to go to. An important one," he stressed for Jazz's benefit. She stuck her tongue out at him from where she'd curled up on the bed, long legs tucked under her insanely hot frilly pink nightie. Yet again talking fell down his list of priorities and his voice sped up. "Can we wrap it up via—"

"What appointment, man? I thought we'd hit a good rhythm today. Lemme guess. You find some other bigger band to work with? Ain't nobody gonna be bigger than The Grunge. Other than Oblivion, of course," he added reluctantly.

Gray had to laugh. "Worst save ever. Actually, no. It's a doctor's appointment. We're finding out our baby's sex tomorrow."

"*Baby?*" Luc growled. "What the actual fuck?"

Gray laughed again. "I told you about Jazz. If you were listening."

"You didn't tell me she was knocked up. Though she is one fine piece of—"

"Dude. Seriously?"

"Sorry. Just stating the obvious."

"Yeah." Gray cleared his throat. One day he'd learn not to get jealous about every man who noticed how gorgeous she was. One day far in the future. "Anyway, we can finish up via email. Or even FaceTime."

"We'll just do it the next day then."

"Nah, I can't. I'm sorry. Turns out I'm gonna be tied up for a while." He licked the inside of his lower lip as Jazz reclined against the pillows, a smile spreading across her face while she slowly parted her legs.

This ridiculously sexy woman wanted to spend more time with him. *That* was what they'd argued about today? Hours, days, weeks he'd never get back if he didn't take them now. She'd been his dream girl for so long, and now she was his.

Fuck work. Just fuck it. It would either be there when he got back or it wouldn't, but he wasn't going to screw up this amazing thing he'd found. Not for anything.

"I'll email you. We'll figure it out," he said over Luc's voice, hitting the end button and tossing the phone aside before he climbed onto the bed.

Her arms lifted to him and he slid into them, fitting himself against her with a groan. Her legs opened, cradling his hips, and her arms encircled his neck as she slanted her mouth over his.

This was what he'd been waiting for, probably his whole godforsaken life. Just this.

He pushed his hands under the silky material, desperate for her skin. The feeling of her all warm and still slightly damp tore another groan from his throat, one that mingled with hers when his fingers closed around her taut nipple. She'd always been so responsive but pregnancy had just turned that up to the nth degree. With a few plucks of his fingers, she was writhing beneath him, her hands streaking down between their bodies to work frantically at his jeans. She shoved them and his boxers down his hips, barely managing to push them below the curve of his ass before she gripped his cock and brought him home.

"Fucking hell," he hissed, and there was no checking his language because she was so hot and wet that his mind blanked out. She fisted him on the first stroke, tightened impossibly on the second. His hips went into overdrive, moving of their own volition while he drove his hands in her hair and his tongue into her mouth. His surges dragged the base of his length over her clit piercing, making his balls draw up night and tight. He had no clue if he was making it good for her, because Christ, he felt like a rutting beast. Mindless. Lost. She was everything, closing him in, enveloping him in heat and light and pleasure. So much pleasure that he couldn't see his way through it to make sure she was there with him too.

Her nails scraped down his back, adding a wicked thrill to the pressure building at the base of his spine. He was already on the verge, a few thrusts away. Sweat blurred into his eyes and he dropped his head, running open-mouthed kisses down her throat. She clenched around him and arched upward, sinking her teeth into his shoulder as the first ripples of her orgasm traveled down his cock. Thank Jesus.

He slid his hand down her hip and between her legs, finding her clit with a speed and accuracy that belied his complete lack of awareness of anything but her spasming pussy. That had become his entire world. Circling his fingers around her clit and her piercing, he found a rhythm that carried her through her initial climax into a second. He pulled back and launched deep, so freaking deep. Forget stars. He saw comets and solar flares. His vision swam, contracting until her flushed cheeks and parted lips and lust-drunk eyes were all he could see.

Trapped within them, he braced a hand on the mattress and pushed into her again and again, letting the undertow of her endless orgasm drag him under.

CHAPTER THREE

Jazz rolled over and glared at the alarm clock. Ten a.m. already? How could that be possible?

She shifted her legs and smiled at the delicious soreness between them. Oh yeah. So *that* was why.

The first time the night before had been quick and unexpected, like heat lightning. Then Gray had shifted into his usual mode, which typically meant a long session between her legs with his mouth before he finished her off with his cock. Was it possible to sprain your tongue? If so, he better be careful, because holy shit.

Her smile grew as she soundlessly swung her legs over the side of the bed and glanced over her shoulder to where he was sprawled on his belly, his face smushed into the pillow. She nearly leaned forward to kiss the smattering of freckles just below his shoulder blade before she caught herself. He needed to sleep too.

Whoa, did he ever after the night they'd put in.

Feeling more than a little smug and a lot happy, she padded into the bathroom to take care of her morning business. The smudges of light bruises around her wrists from his hands were like badges of honor. The reddened areas on her throat from his evening scruff were even better. She knew she'd find more of the same between her thighs.

Makeup hid the worst of the marks and helped with the dark shadows under her eyes. Perhaps she could sneak in a nap later. If she really was done at the studio, she might actually get a whole day off.

Despite what Gray had said, she wouldn't plan on spending it with him. He had important stuff to do. He was making time for their appointment, and that was plenty. Anything else was just gravy.

She headed to their closet and bypassed the couple of maternity tops she'd bought several times before she decided why not? So she technically didn't need to wear them yet. She wanted to. She pulled on a pair of denim shorts and the flowing white top with flowers embroidered around the collar and hem. It was super girly, not really her usual style, but maybe that was part of the whole new attitude she had going on.

Some changes were good. If she just managed to tone down the Pregzilla part a bit, she'd be happy.

A quick glance at the bed informed her than Gray was still dead to the world. She beelined downstairs for the kitchen, unsurprised to find it empty. The other boys in the house rarely dragged themselves out before noon. Fine by her. She'd happily enjoy her wheat toast and raspberry jam in peace.

The doorbell chimed before she'd even made it to the table with her plate of food. She frowned down at it as her belly rumbled. "Sorry, baby. No eats yet. Coming," she called, noticing her bottle of prenatal vitamins on the counter again. What the hell. Simon was going to grow a third boob if he didn't stop chowing down on those like they were candy. It was probably her fault for getting the gummy version, but jeez.

She set down her breakfast and grabbed her vitamins so she didn't forget to hide them from Simon and aimed for the front door. She reached it just as it chimed again. "Who is it?" she asked, pulling the door open anyway because she was a little too used to living with a bunch of big strapping boys who could defend or destroy if need be.

Who waited on the doorstep posed no physical threat to her well-being, but her mental and emotional health was anyone's guess.

"Mrs. Duffy." Jazz swallowed hard, her gaze drifting over the other woman from the top of coiffed dark hair to the tips of her polished pumps. She wore her typical country club chic, right down to the pastels and pearls. "This is...unexpected."

Mrs. Duffy's stilted smile lasted until her focus dropped below the neck. "Jasmine. You look—" Her gaze shot back up to her face and held. "Pregnant. Oh my, it's true."

"You knew? How did you know?" Almost as soon as she asked the question, Jazz answered the question for herself.

The frigging tabloids.

They'd yet to make an official announcement yet, though the rumors were running rampant and it was pretty much the worse kept secret in the rock world. Well, probably not. Lots of other way more important people than them tried and failed to keep big stuff under wraps. And they weren't even trying that hard. Gray had obviously told that guy in The Grunge yesterday, and—

And Gray's mother was staring at her with tears in her eyes. Oh God.

"You're wearing a maternity top." Mrs. Duffy grabbed her hand. "These are prenatal vitamins. That only means one thing."

"Not necessarily." As gently as possible, she detangled herself from Gray's mother's death grip. "Simon keeps taking them and he's not with child. We all hope."

"I saw an article yesterday at the store. I didn't believe it at first. Surely Gray would call if—" She pinched her lips together and shook her head. "I'm sorry. My emotions are just getting the better of me. May I come in?"

Jazz blinked. What was happening here? The last time she'd talked to Mrs. Duffy, she hadn't exactly been apologizing and fluttering. She'd been angry and blaming Jazz for everything that had gone wrong with her relationship with her sons, not to mention their relationship with each other. It had even seemed like Mrs. Duffy held Jazz at least partially responsible for Gray's older brother Brent's suicide, though Jazz hadn't had contact with him in years. Now she was politely asking to come inside?

Harper's voice sounded in her head, as if she was standing right behind Jazz. *Dummy, she wants access to her grandchild. You are the keeper of the baby. Hello, power position.*

Could it be that simple? Not that she had any intention of keeping her child from his or her grandparents. She and Gray had already had that discussion, but she'd left the ball in his court as far as reaching out again to his parents and telling them the news.

Now the ball had pinged firmly back onto Jazz's side, and she had no clue whether to serve, volley or duck.

"Um, sure. Please do." She stepped back to allow Mrs. Duffy room to enter. "Would you like some coffee or tea?"

She shut the door and frowned. Fuck, they didn't *have* any coffee or tea. None of them would touch tea, in spite of the doctor suggesting a herbal one for Jazz to try to help her sleep, and Nick was the coffee drinker, but he needed to make a grocery run. She should've grabbed some for him last night. Now she had nothing to serve for guests.

For her soon-to-be mother-in-law. Lord help her.

"No, thank you. Do you have orange juice?" Mrs. Duffy pivoted on her heels, her gaze lowering to Jazz's belly once again. "I imagine you do. It's a good thing to give the baby. All that vitamin C."

"We're out of juice now. I do have some orange Kool-Aid—" She stopped at the horror that flashed across Mrs. Duffy's face.

She could almost hear Mrs. Duffy's internal dialogue now. *You're poisoning my grandchild with additives and sugar!*

"It's sugar-free," she added weakly, feeling utterly stupid and small.

She waited for the sonic boom to come. Any moment now, Mrs. Duffy would flash her forked tongue and demand to know why the heck she thought she had any business getting pregnant when it was obvious she was barely capable of taking care of herself.

Right then, Jazz was tempted to agree with her.

Gray's mother swallowed deeply and plastered an utterly insincere smile on her flawlessly made-up face. "Orange was always my favorite flavor."

Yet again Jazz was reduced to blinking and gaping. *Oh my word.*

"Um, okay. The kitchen is this way," Jazz said, hurrying past her and down the hall.

Then she came to a halt, looking around as if she'd never seen the place before. What was she supposed to do now?

Duh, give the woman a drink and act hospitable. Play hostess. You can do that. You've been playing different roles all your life.

Spying her forgotten breakfast, Jazz tried to smile. "Would you like some toast and jam? Or fresh fruit? I do have that. I have watermelon and red grapes and a slightly overripe cantaloupe. There might even be grapefruit left."

Mrs. Duffy smiled thinly. "Just the...Kool-Aid, please."

Jazz nodded and hurried to the fridge. This sure felt like that old adage about drinking the Kool-Aid. They were both pretending to be civil when there was all this crap seething under the surface, just waiting to explode all over the—*oh shit*—really dusty kitchen floor.

Ignoring the dust for the time being, she poured the orange drink into the only clean glass she could find and handed it to Gray's mom. Then she frowned at the full sink of dishes. Damn dirty boys.

"The maid's on vacation," she said as cheerfully as possible when Mrs. Duffy's gaze drifted toward the sink. "It's so hard finding good help these days."

Mr. and Mrs. Duffy actually did have a maid. Gray had grown up with one in the house. The Duffys had money with a capital M, but they didn't like to be flashy about it. Instead they used it to do good things like bring poor little foster children into their home so they could get attached to the Duffys before they were cast back onto the street like the pathetic urchins they were.

Or had been once, in her case. She wasn't an urchin or a foster child any longer. She was a drummer in a band, and a mother-to-be, and soon she would be a wife.

It looked like she might get a chance to be a sister too.

The older woman gave no indication of getting Jazz's sarcasm. "Do you truly have a maid? If so, good for you. I imagine a nanny is next? I have some recommendations that could help. Several of my friends have children who—"

"A nanny? Why?"

"Because you won't be able to take care of the child on your own. You simply can't." Mrs. Duffy lifted the glass, gave it a dark look and drained it in nearly one gulp. "You can't," she added for good measure.

Jazz dropped into the nearest chair. "Why not?"

"You're in a band. You keep horrible hours. You go on tour. How could you possibly care for a child while you're traveling around the world?"

"We haven't done a world tour yet," Jazz muttered. "We have a bus. We can bring the baby. We've already talked about it. It won't even be just us. Harper and Deacon are having a baby too, so our kids will be able to play together."

God, she wished Deak or Harp were there to talk to Mrs. Duffy. They were both so much better at projecting a stable image than she was. But Harp had an early job today and Deak had gone with her to help. That meant Jazz was on her own with the rest of the misfits.

And today she felt like she was leading the misfit brigade.

Mrs. Duffy clutched her pearls. Literally. "One baby on a smelly, dirty bus isn't enough? You're shoehorning in two?" She shook her head and set down her glass with a firm *clink*. "And Grayson is onboard with this plan?"

"Grayson," Gray said smoothly, entering the room, "not only is onboard with it, he was the first one to suggest how it could work. Hello, Mother." He walked past the woman in question and headed right for Jazz, brushing a kiss over her head before sliding his arm possessively around her shoulders. "What brings you here?"

Mrs. Duffy's face lit up as she drank down the sight of the son she hadn't seen in years with all of the zeal she hadn't shown while consuming the Kool-Aid. "Grayson," she whispered, the gray eyes so like her youngest son's filling anew. "You look good."

"Did you expect me not to?"

"Of course not. It's just...the last time I saw you, you were in the hospital."

Gray's arm tightened almost imperceptibly around Jazz's shoulders. "Yes, I was. But that was months ago and I'm fine now. All healed, clean and sober." He paused. "Did the check I send you not clear?"

In spite of the issues she'd had with Gray's parents in the past, it was hard for Jazz to watch Mrs. Duffy's face crumple in on itself at the question. "Do you honestly think we care? You're our son. We want to provide for you. We missed out on so much." Her gaze shot to Jazz for one thrumming moment before returning to Gray. "The money doesn't matter."

"It does to me. I appreciate your help at a difficult time for me. For us," he added, rubbing the top of Jazz's arm under her ruffled sleeve. "But we're doing fine now. We'll be okay."

"*This* is your idea of okay?" Mrs. Duffy set her purse on her lap and removed a folded paper. As she smoothed it out on the table, Jazz saw it was a tabloid.

Oh God.

"If that video wasn't enough, now they're talking about some love triangle within the band." She arched an eyebrow in a way that made Jazz unintentionally retreat into the chair, which only made Gray's arm tighten that much more around her shoulders. "Between the racy videos and long tours on cramped buses, never mind the...questionable other members, what kind of environment is this to raise a baby?"

"Excuse me, I couldn't help but overhear," Nick said from the doorway.

"Here we go," Gray muttered as Nick strolled into the room, looking rumpled in his wrinkled Ninja Turtles pajama bottoms and a worn thin T-shirt.

Ninja Turtles? Obviously he hadn't had a girl over the night before, since they hadn't heard any uproarious laughter at his attire. Then again, she couldn't have heard much beyond her own screams.

"I'd like to alleviate your concerns on one level, Mrs. Duffy." Nick gestured with his coffee mug. What he had in it, Jazz had no idea since she highly doubted he'd gone shopping on his own. "There is no love triangle. Never was."

Jazz tipped back her head and caught Gray's eye. He jerked a shoulder, as perplexed as she was.

One never knew what Nick would say from one minute to the next. He could be your biggest enemy or your best friend, depending on his mood.

"Oh, is that so? And you would know that how?"

"Because I'm supposed to be in it. But nope. No triangles. Just a circle with those two." He swiveled his fingers in Jazz and Gray's direction. "Anyone with a pair of eyes can see no one else has a chance with either of them."

Mrs. Duffy's eyes narrowed. "What kind of love triangle was this?"

Jazz snorted, triggering Gray to cough into his hand. Nick didn't look so amused. He'd tried to help and somehow made it seem more salacious.

"There is no love triangle," Jazz said when she was sure she wouldn't burst into inappropriate giggles. "We're engaged. Nick is...Nick."

"That about sums it up." He saluted with his mug as Simon sauntered into the room rocking some serious bedhead.

Simon went straight to the counter, fumbled around and frowned. "Hey, where's my candy?"

"It's not your candy, those are my vitamins." Spying them on the table where she'd put them down, she grabbed them and shoved them in her shorts pocket. "Unless you have something to tell us, you should not be taking them."

"But look at my hair. It's so shiny." He fluffed it with one hand before swiveling on his bare feet and apparently realizing they had a guest. "Well, hello. Mrs. Duffy, is it? I remember you from that unfortunate time in the hospital." Before Mrs. Duffy had a chance to respond, Simon moved forward to lift her hand to his lips. "You look absolutely lovely. Pink is your color."

Mrs. Duffy actually blushed. "Why, thank you."

"She's married, Simon," Gray said drily.

"So? Looking is free, and I can't help admiring beautiful scenery." He smiled and stepped back.

"You're too kind, Simon," Mrs. Duffy said, still blushing like a schoolgirl.

"I only speak the truth."

"To her and every other female within earshot." Jazz shook her head and glanced at her watch. "Oh crap. We're running late. We need to get ready to go." She glanced back at Gray and noticed he'd just pulled on sweatpants. "Go get dressed," she said, elbowing him.

Nick pulled out a chair and grabbed Mrs. Duffy's tabloid, paging through it despite her stare. "Late for what?"

"We're going to the doctor's to find out—ouch, what?" Jazz broke off when Gray pinched her upper arm, her gaze following his to his mother.

Whoops.

Mrs. Duffy leaned forward on her chair like a sprinter about to hit the ground running. "You're going to the doctor? Is the baby okay?"

"The baby is fine."

"*All* of the babies are fine." Nick turned the tabloid around to view something from another angle, probably a pair of boobs. "We're going to be overrun with them. It's like a damn VH-1 show gone wrong."

"They don't belong on a bus."

Nick held up his hands, palms out. "No arguments here. Babies don't belong in a band, period, but no one checked with me before reproducing. So yanno, you deal."

"Babies also don't belong around drugs and alcohol—"

"Stop right there," Gray said quietly. "The only one who's had a problem with drugs in this band is me, and I've been to rehab. I'm trying every day not to get sucked back into where I was, and they're doing their part to help. More than they should be asked to do, truthfully. There's not a joint or a single bottle of alcohol in this house. Go check." He crossed his arms. "I dare you."

His mother set her jaw. "If that's so, I commend them."

"Yeah, like you commend me for being a user in the first place."

"We all make mistakes," she said, glancing away.

Simon cleared his throat. "Speaking of mistakes, I may have a flask hidden in my room. You know, maybe." He leaned a hip on the table and made a show of stealing the magazine from Nick. "Oh hey, is that another love triangle story? Damn, you guys get all the good press."

Mrs. Duffy aimed another pointed look at Jazz and Gray and said nothing.

As the silence extended, and Gray made no move to get dressed, Jazz gave in and offered an olive branch. If she didn't, they'd never get to the doctor's. "You can come with us if you want. We're supposed to find out the baby's sex. Well, if the kid stops jumping around. Last time they tried to check he or she wasn't in the right position—"

"I'm sure she's too busy," Gray said, tugging Jazz to her feet. "Let's go get dressed."

"Hello, I am dressed." Jazz glanced down at her clothes. "What's wrong with how I look?"

"Female pity party commences now," Nick said in an undertone.

"You look just fine, Peach Parfait. In fact, you're overdressed in my book. Feel free to lose the shorts. Or the top. Both?"

Everyone ignored Simon, as usual.

Mrs. Duffy stood. "I'd like to come along to the doctor, if that's okay with you."

Gray's hand tensed around Jazz's forearm. "What purpose would that serve?"

"Gray," Jazz admonished, casting him a narrow-eyed look. But his attention remained strictly focused on his mother while he flexed his jaw.

"I'm your mother. This is still my grandchild, no matter what you think of me."

"I think the bigger problem is how you feel about us."

"I love you, you know that." Mrs. Duffy's voice broke. "What did I ever do to make you doubt that?"

"Want a list?" He pulled Jazz against his chest and caged her in with his arms as he turned them both to face Mrs. Duffy. "Top of it was when you made me choose her over you. I may be a former drug addict and a current asshole, but I'll tell you this much—my kid will never have to choose between me and someone they love. Someone whose only crime was loving him back."

Jazz shut her eyes against the prickle that heralded an oncoming onslaught. "Let her come with us," she whispered, not sure he could hear her over the wild beat of her heart.

He braced, tension leaking from the arms holding her safe. "You can't honestly want that."

"I do." She opened her eyes and met Mrs. Duffy's gaze. The gratitude she saw reflected on her face strengthened her voice. "She's lost a lot too."

Gray released her and stepped back. He pushed a hand through his shaggy dark hair and turned away. "As you wish."

Jazz watched him leave, a lump in her throat.

"Thank you," Mrs. Duffy said quietly. "You don't know how much this means."

Jazz said nothing, just picked up her plate of cold food and took it into the living room to eat in the quiet. She'd probably made a mistake by trying to smooth things over.

Another mistake. The list was growing by the hour.

Gray stared at the ultrasound monitor while the doctor prattled on about statistics and vital signs and more information than he could ever possibly have a hope of retaining. The most salient point was on the tiny screen in front of him.

Jazz had an actual baby inside her. Not in theory, not someday far in the future. Now. She was carrying his baby, and that baby had its leg up just high enough for them to see the very obvious equipment between his legs.

His. They were having a boy.

His mother was asking a million questions, as usual. Did everything seem okay? Was the pregnancy proceeding according to schedule? And Jazz kept pulling at her paper gown and swallowing loudly, a sure sign she was about to cry. She'd always hated crying, and before the last few months, he could've counted on one hand how many times he'd seen her with tears in her eyes. Lately it seemed to be a near-constant thing.

Right then, he understood. They were having a fucking baby.

By the time he led her out a short time later, she'd given into full-scale sniffling and his mother had lapsed into silence. Since he hadn't come out of his own fog yet, he couldn't even summon any annoyance that his mother was there—or that Jazz had overruled his thoughts on the subject. None of that mattered.

Only one thing did. He glanced at Jazz as she dried her cheeks and swallowed hard. Two things.

His kid, and his wife.

He waited until his mom slipped into the backseat of the car and shut the door. Then he turned Jazz toward him and gripped her elbows until she lifted her face to his. The sunshine illuminated the faint tracks on her cheeks, making them glisten. He wanted to kiss them away. To make sure she never had another reason to cry anything but happy tears for the rest of her life.

"You're done in the studio." It wasn't a question. It was a low statement deliberately said beneath the hearing range of his mother closed inside the car.

Sensing the urgency of his mood, Jazz nodded. "Yes."

"Does Harper have a catering job tomorrow?"

"I don't know."

"Call her and find out."

"Why?"

He couldn't help but smile at the suspicion in her voice. "Because we're going to meet your sister and she should be there."

Jazz frowned. "We're going now to meet Molly?"

He nodded. "No time better than the present, right? You heard me tell Luc that I'd be unavailable for a few days."

"Yeah," Jazz said slowly, "but why does Harper need to be there?"

"Moral support."

"But I have you."

Her simple response caused the tightness to return to his throat. He smiled through it, his thumbs circling on the insides of her elbows. "Yeah, you do. I just think Harper should be there too."

"We're just driving up for the day, right?"

"Honey, we both know a day won't be enough."

Jazz glanced at the ground then lifted her head, a smile playing around her mouth. "You know me too well."

"Just ask Harper if she can come up overnight with us. If need be, I'll drive her back the next day and you can stay with your sister until I get back."

"My sister." The tears were back in her eyes, and this time, they weren't merely happy. "God, I'm not sure I'm ready for this. It's not just about seeing her. If my mom's there too..."

"We'll cross that bridge together. Call Harper," he said, rounding the car to slip into the driver's side.

Just as he expected, Jazz leaned against the door and placed her call. He'd banked on her not wanting to make it in front of his mother, which played right into his hands.

"You really claim to love me?" he asked in an undertone, facing straight ahead.

"How can you ask that?" His mother huffed out a breath. "Of course I do. Your father does too. You're all we have left. You and the baby—"

"And Jazz," he interrupted. "You don't get me or that kid without her. She's the only reason you're here right now. Remember that."

His mother fell silent.

He flexed his fingers around the steering wheel, speaking quickly as Jazz laughed loudly outside the car. Her distraction was perfect timing. "I need your help."

"Whatever you need," his mother said quickly enough to stir the guilt he hadn't realized he had left in her direction. He'd buried it under anger and hurt and resolve so many years ago that he'd figured it had ebbed away entirely.

"We're driving to San Jose to meet Jazz's sister today. Tomorrow I need you to get the band to San Francisco. I'll tell you the exact location in a couple hours after I make some calls." He met her gaze in the rearview mirror. "Can you do that for me?"

Her lips trembled before they firmed. "You're going to marry her."

"Yes."

He waited for her to tell him he was making a mistake. That he needed to take time to think, to allow the emotion that had arisen from the doctor's visit to fade before he made rash decisions he couldn't take back.

Instead she nodded and gave him a small smile. "I can do that."

He sucked in a breath. "Thank you."

"You're my son."

He didn't give the words a chance to take root inside him where they could weaken the walls he'd constructed so carefully. "And Lila," he said, increasing his grip on the wheel. "She should be there too. Harper will probably ride up with us."

"Okay. I'll take care of it." She didn't offer any appeals for herself or his father, and that was what broke him.

"You and Dad can come too," he said finally, forcing himself to open his eyes. Hers were damp and riveted to the reflection of his in the rearview mirror. "If you want," he added when she didn't speak.

"*If* we want?" She laughed brokenly. "Oh Gray. Being part of your life is all we want."

Jazz pulled open the door and cast a wary glance at the backseat before slipping into the passenger seat.

"Well?" he demanded.

"She has a job tonight. She's really sorry."

"What about tomorrow? Is she busy then?"

"I'm not sure." She peered at him closely. Too closely. "Are you okay?"

"I'm fine. Never mind. We'll figure it out." He snapped on his belt and reversed too swiftly, belatedly realizing she was still staring at him and hadn't belted herself in yet. "Put on your seatbelt."

"I would have, if you hadn't dislocated my neck from my spinal column back there." Shaking her head, she snapped her belt into place. "What is your deal? You're acting seriously weird. Is it the baby thing?" She sighed. "I know you wanted a girl. Are you disappointed?"

"Disappointed? Are you fucking kidding me?"

"Gray," his mother said. "Language, please."

"Yes. Little ears," Jazz reminded him, cupping her stomach as if he'd forgotten who she was referring to.

"No, I'm not disappointed." He struggled to keep his voice even as he finished backing out of the spot and drove out of the lot. "I told you I'd be happy with either one."

"I know."

He gave her a sidelong glance. "Are you disappointed?"

"Oh God, no. I'm thrilled beyond belief for a boy. They're so much fun. I bet he'll look just like you. He's already very— athletic," she said, wiggling her brows in a way that indicated she wasn't talking about sports.

"Hmm. That is true. But you've got some flexibility going yourself."

Her mouth twitched as she tried not to grin. "Besides, Harper was right. I'll just keep trying until I get my girl."

His mother made a choked sound in the back, and for once, he didn't get annoyed. He just laughed. "Is that so? Do I have a say in the matter?"

"Sure. You can say yes."

He laughed again and reached across the console for her hand, cupping it against her belly. "When it comes to you, I don't know any other word."

CHAPTER FOUR

When she'd mentioned wanting to visit Molly as soon as possible, she hadn't meant *this*.

After heading back to the house to say goodbye to Gray's mother—who had seemed unnaturally misty-eyed, which might have been a byproduct of the ultrasound appointment or just that day's smog activity—and to pack a couple of bags, they were on the road again to San Jose. About an hour into the trip, Jazz came to two conclusions.

They hadn't called Molly to ascertain she was willing to see them so soon. Or hell, that she would even be home.

And she was hungry. Seriously freaking hungry.

The second issue was solved with a quick detour through the drive-thru, though she was guilted into getting a salad with her chocolate shake. Not that she cared. Even wilted lettuce under fat free dressing tasted absolutely glorious.

The first issue involved a phone call that had Jazz's now sated belly crawling with nerves as the phone rang.

"Hello? Who's this?"

Jazz inhaled sharply at the sound of the girl's rich, alto voice, causing Gray to look her way in obvious alarm. She waved him off. "Hello, Molly? Is this Molly?"

"Yes. Who is this?"

"It's Jazz." She cleared her throat. "I mean, Mine."

"Mine?" Molly repeated, as if the word didn't quite make sense. Because it didn't. What kind of nickname was Mine? But then Molly laughed, and Jazz relaxed in her seat. "Oh wow, Mine. I just remembered that. I used to call you Mine."

"Yes, you did."

"Wow."

Silence hummed over the line and Jazz bit her lip, wondering what to say next. "Um, I got your letter. We're on our way to come see you. If that's okay."

"Really? Like now?"

"Yes. We're a few hours away."

"Oh shit. I mean, yeah, that's great. I just—I need to clean up. Like a lot. Um, can you call before you get here?"

"That's what this is." Jazz laughed weakly. "I'm calling ahead to let you know we're on the way."

"Oh. Right. That's cool. I mean, can you call when you're about an hour away? I'm kind of busy right now but I want to make sure to shovel out the place before you arrive."

"Where's Mom? Can't she help?"

"Nah, I'm good. Anyhoo, thanks for the heads up. See ya soon, sis. Bye!"

The phone went dead.

Jazz reached for her chocolate shake and took a quick drink to wet her dry throat. God, she was so nervous she was practically shaking. Molly was her sister. Her flesh and blood. She had absolutely no reason to be anxious. She could practically see the Oprah-style tearful family reunion unfolding now.

"Well? What did she say?"

Jazz wiped her mouth and stuck her now empty cup back into the holder. Why hadn't she gotten a large? A small hadn't been nearly enough. In fact, she wanted to keep drinking that cool chocolatey goodness until she floated away on—

"Jazz? Hello?"

"Sorry. She was perfectly polite. She seemed delighted we were on the way."

Molly had said she was busy. That was probably why she wasn't more excited. She had to 'shovel out' the place, and no one looked forward to cleaning.

"She was pleasant," she added into the silence. "Very much so."

"So you've said, several times. Which means to me that she wasn't 'delighted' at all."

"Don't be a jerk. I'm still hungry, by the way."

Unsurprisingly, he ignored her plantive request for food. "What did she say?"

"Not much. She was busy. We should've given her more noticed or hell, even called to ask if she was ready for visitors. It was wrong to fucking assume."

He lifted a brow. "Language there, Sailor Boy."

It was her turn to ignore him. "I mean, it was probably presumptuous on our part. Just because she sent a letter and said she missed me and wanted to get to know me, that didn't mean right away. Hey, there's a chicken place. Let's go there."

"If we get off the freeway again, we're going to get stuck in rush hour traffic."

"Okay. Do you think they have bourbon chicken?" Jazz gazed longingly out the window at the passing billboard. "The baby wants chicken. It's not me."

"Right." He leaned forward and opened the glove box, then tossed an ancient granola bar in her lap. "Eat that. I'm not getting off the freeway again unless you want to turn around and go home."

"Okay. Let's do that."

"Jazz. What aren't you telling me?"

"Nothing. It's just..." She sighed and tore at the wrapper of the granola bar she had zippo interest in. "This doesn't feel like an Oprah reunion, and I kind of had my heart set on one." She bit into her snack and nearly broke a tooth, but she kept eating it anyway because at least it contained crusty chocolate chips. "Harper's right. I'm an idiot."

He frowned. "Harper calls you an idiot? I thought she was your best friend."

"She is. And she doesn't say that exact word, but I am. She thinks I'm too soft. Basically a runny egg who never buys a clue."

"Yeah, I'm not following this conversation at all." He grabbed his iPhone and flipped it to a metal track, turning it up until she could barely think.

She hit the off button. "Sorry. I'm not in the mood for music. You know what I *am* in the mood for, though?"

"Let me guess. Chicken?"

"Yes."

"Talk to me." He slid his arm along the back of her seat to play with the ends of her ponytails. She'd tied one off on both sides of her head in deference to the climbing heat that didn't seem to be alleviated by the rattling A/C. Or else her internal thermometer was off.

Maybe it was hunger sweats, caused by too much salad and not enough red meat.

"I am talking to you."

"She didn't seem happy we were coming, did she?"

She forced herself to stare straight ahead, because if she met his gaze, she would probably crumble. And she was frigging sick and tired of being a hormonal mess. "There is no *we* in this case. The one she didn't seem all that thrilled to see is me."

"I bet she was just surprised is all. She probably figured she'd get a letter in return, not a visit. At least not right away."

"I'm sure you're right. It's fine. Everything is fine."

"What happens if it's not?" he asked, so softly that she almost couldn't make out what he said over the hum of the air conditioner.

"Then I go through the same sense of loss all over again," she answered, just as softly. Knowing he could hear her even when she didn't have the breath left to raise her voice. "I'm back there walking away from the only family I've ever known, not knowing when I'll ever see them again. Rewriting the end isn't possible. This is just...it."

"You have another family now."

"I know." She reached up to hold his hand against her shoulder, turning her cheek into the familiar comfort he always gave her, no matter what. "That's why I'm strong enough to see this through. Why I'm not screaming for you to turn the car around in case this is just going to make things worse."

"How could it be worse?"

"Oh, it could be." She let out a brittle laugh. "If I don't go see her, I can pretend that she's still a little girl who isn't old enough to decide she wants me in her life."

He didn't speak for a long moment, splitting his gaze between her and the road. His brow was marred with lines, a sure sign he was concerned. "We don't have to go to her place if you don't want to. I'll just keep driving until we get to San Francisco."

She didn't have to ask him if he was serious. He would do it, if she asked him to. He'd just keep driving forever if it would make her happy.

"What's in San Francisco?"

He flashed her a distracted smile. "A chance to rewrite history."

"Hmm. Very mysterious." She leaned across the console to kiss his jaw. "Just so you know, I'd be down with a Motel Six. Turns out the second trimester is when a chick gets really horny. Just FYI."

"*Gets* really horny? Did I miss the time when you weren't horny?" He laughed as she pushed his arm. "Not that I have a problem with this. Not one bit."

"Watch it or I'll go back to whining for chicken."

"You want chicken more than my dick?"

"Depends what kind of dressing is on it. And what kind of sides. If we're talking buttery corn on the cob or some creamy coleslaw—" She laughed as he covered her mouth with his hand, but she didn't let up. "Maybe a biscuit. I could even go for some green beans..." Playfully, she nipped his palm.

"I love that sound," he said, dropping his hand to her thigh. He rubbed it while he switched lanes, his attention now firmly back on the road.

She had to stop distracting him with talk of chicken and sex. Either topic made her entirely too excitable.

"What sound?"

"You, laughing. You don't do it nearly enough."

"Sure I do. I laughed this morning when I saw the kid had a twig and two berries." She grinned. "It was pretty funny to see your jaw hit the ground."

"Yeah, yeah. Watch it, Edwards."

"You won't be able to call me that once my last name is Duffy." When that would happen, she wasn't exactly sure. They hadn't firmed up wedding plans yet, because they were waiting to see how the album release went and the booking for the tour. Their schedule over the next few months was so packed that even a short honeymoon would be hard to pull off.

"That might be happening sooner than you think."

"Huh?" She frowned, jarring herself out of hazy daydreams of wedding dresses and seven-layer cakes. Truthfully, the seven-layer cake appealed to her more than getting all done up just to prance down the aisle like a polo pony, but she wasn't about to eschew tradition.

"Nothing." He yawned, but she had the strangest feeling that he was faking it. Who fake-yawned? And why? "I'm exhausted, since someone didn't let me get any sleep last night." He flashed her a sexy grin. "I think you should sing to me to keep me awake."

"Dream on, rockstar. But if you ease your seat back a bit, I have an idea for another way I could keep you awake."

Shooting her a look, he slowed down for a fraction of a second and did as she asked. "Do tell."

"I was always a show kind of girl." She undid her seatbelt and edged closer to flip open the button of his jeans.

"You do realize that this is against vehicular law. You're not wearing your seatbelt. And crawling—oh sweet fuck. I'm supposed to be responsible."

She freed him from his jeans and boxers, grinning to herself over that silly *this way to Oblivion* tattoo that he'd gotten while high last winter, and rubbed her thumb over the rounded tip. He wasn't hard yet but she knew just what to do to get him there fast.

"No, you're supposed to keep your eyes on the road and your hands on the wheel. Let me take care of this." She gripped him in one hand and slicked her tongue up the side, turning her head so she could look up at his strong profile, highlighted by the sun streaming through the windows. He flicked her a glance, his jaw going tight under the beginnings of his five o'clock shadow. "It's my job, and I'm damn good at it."

"Your job is to suck me off?"

"Mmm-hmm. Among others. And right now, yours is to sit there and take it without letting anyone know what I'm doing." She twisted her neck and eyed the steering wheel. "Can that thing be raised any higher?"

He played with the levers and gave her a triumphant grin. "We're in luck. It was stuck in the middle position."

Not so much luck. It gave her little room to work, but she was small...and persistent.

"You're definitely getting lucky," she agreed, slipping back to grab her purse.

The dejection that flashed across his face was priceless. "Then why'd you go back over there?"

"Patience, my sweet." She pried open the mint case in her purse and slipped one in her mouth before resuming her position. "Go faster. I like it when you speed."

"I'm already doing the speed limit. I will not go—Jesus," he hissed as her cool lips slid over the tip of his cock. She pressed the mint against the head, swirling it around to add that extra bit of sensation before she wiggled closer and took him deeper.

The car sped up, just as requested.

She sucked harder, using the nails on her free hand to tease his balls. She shifted onto her knees, flattening her torso to wriggle into better position. In a couple months she wouldn't be able to do this.

Hell, if she'd had that burger with lunch, she probably wouldn't be able to do this. Her shorts already felt suspiciously snug.

She slid her lips up and down his shaft, both hands working, drawing him slightly to the side so she didn't get her head stuck under the wheel. That thought made her swallow a giggle and the sound rippled over his length, causing him to remove one hand from the wheel to fist it in her hair.

"Sorry." He sounded choked. Completely breathless. "Can't stop."

Her only response was another guttural noise in her throat as she cupped his balls tighter, rolling the underside of her engagement ring over the sensitive flesh to increase the friction. Some men might not've enjoyed that kind of play, but Gray sure did. His fingers weaved through her hair, pulling on her scalp as he forced her subtly down on his dick. Her clit pulsed at show of dominance and she squirmed, pressing her thighs together.

"You're getting wet for me," he breathed.

She pulled back long enough to roll her tongue over the pearly drop of fluid she'd earned on the head of hic cock. "So wet. I'm going to have to change my shorts before we get there."

"Christ. I'm going to make a fucking mess if you keep talking like that."

"That's what my mouth is for."

Lightly, he drummed his fist on the wheel. "Fuck. I can't focus on the road."

"Yes, you can. And stop swearing or I stop blowing your mind." At his low curse, she drew him back inside, taking him in until the quick burn of tears blurred her eyes. She pushed on, relaxing her throat, hollowing her cheeks. Caressing his balls with one hand, she hummed softly, unintentionally picking up the beat to "Sugar Kiss." His hips rolled up to meet her, taking her past her comfort zone to where there was only him. He slammed on the brakes, swore, and she didn't move. Just kept sucking for all she was worth.

He would never let her be hurt. Never risk her or the baby for a moment. And right now she was about to prove her appreciation.

She squeezed her hand around the base of his shaft, adding the scrape of nails that always shoved him close to the point of oblivion. Then she pulled him to the side again away from the wheel and drew her head up, letting the trails of his desire cling to her lips before she smoothed them back down his cock. Slowly engulfing him again and again while he swelled and throbbed in her mouth.

"I have to come," he rasped, and she couldn't nod fast enough. She wanted him on her tongue, in her throat.

When she faced her past, she wanted to taste him everywhere and know she was his.

His erection jerked in her hand and she closed her fingers like a vise, making his thighs bunch and flex under her upper body. "Goddamn, baby." He hit the gas again and she had the sensation of speed and the breeze wafting through the crack in the window before the car zagged left and hot fluid pumped into her mouth.

She took down every drop, swallowing over and over while her hand prolonged the rhythm on his pulsing flesh. And then when she was done, she pulled back long enough to suck in a breath before going back down to lick him clean. It was only then that she realized he was panting like he'd run a race and his knee was jittering like he couldn't keep it still.

"You okay?" she asked, lifting his T-shirt to nibble along his sexy happy trail. God, his body was a damn feast to behold. She could lose herself on this particular playground for years.

A lifetime.

He didn't answer for so long that she shifted to look up at him. He was grinning, his gaze centered on the road. His thumb circled at her temple before sliding down her cheek to rub over her swollen lips. "You're a fucking goddess. Freaking," he amended when she started to correct him.

"Finally, the man is learning." She shifted back onto her seat and rolled her neck like a prizefighter who'd just emerged victorious after a title bout. "So...chicken?"

He laughed and turned on his signal to get off at the next exit.

She snapped on her seatbelt and grinned. No matter the odds, she never gave up.

That meant she wouldn't give up on her little sister either. Maybe Oprah wouldn't be hiding behind the drapes with a camera crew just yet, but she could still make this into a happy ending. She refused to settle for anything less.

Gray stood in the outside hallway of the restaurant, phone in hand, while Jazz bobbed her head to the country music coming through the speakers and pulled off crispy pieces of breading. She popped them into her mouth and licked her fingers, making him fight a grin. How the hell could she be so adorable not thirty minutes after swallowing his come like a damn porn star?

Better than a porn star. Not that he'd watched that much porn, all things considered, but no woman could be hotter than Jazz. The fact that she'd crawled all over their car on her hands and knees while carrying their baby in her belly...yeah.

He shifted and gripped the phone tighter. He was getting hard again, just from watching her eat chicken. Fuck.

"This is Father Freeley. My secretary said you have a rush job."

Gray sent up a quick apology for the timing of this phone call. He was a lapsed Catholic in all ways, but this was pushing it even for him. "Yes, I do. I was referred to you from—well, it's kind of a long story, but you used to work at Holy Family in Vista View. You were one of the priests who baptized me."

"Was I now? How long ago was that?"

"More than twenty years ago."

"And now you're getting married."

"Yes, well, I hope to. I didn't really plan anything ahead of time."

"Well, then. I hope you're not treating your marriage the same way. I'm all for spur-of-the-moment, but if you haven't gone through the suggested pre-marital counseling—"

"We've been in love for close to a decade. I'm not backing out."

Father Freeley let out a long breath. "You're still young, son. What's the rush? Why not take the time to give your bride—and you—the wedding of your dreams?"

Gray looked through the glass door where Jazz was now tapping her fingers on the tabletop while she sipped on her iced tea. He smiled. She did that whenever she was bored. Drummer's curse. In a minute, she'd probably come out here to look for him. The bathroom excuse only worked for so long.

"I'm hoping I can pull that off in about twenty-four hours. We're not high-maintenance people. We don't really care about the ceremony, we just want to be married. Need to be."

"She's pregnant, isn't she?"

Gray coughed. "Uh—"

Father Freeley laughed. "Son, you're not the first nor will you be the last to call me in a panic about a rush ceremony. Is she about to give birth?"

"No. Not even close. She's barely showing yet, and besides, that's not why I want to do it now. We're going on tour soon and with the album coming out, it's just going to be too hard to find time to get away."

"Album, hmm? This is starting not to sound like the usual couple I assist in these times."

"We're in a band."

"I figured that. Don't suppose you're in the Christian music field?"

"No." Gray thought of Oblivion's current hit "Sugar Kiss"—aka an ode to oral sex, specifically oral sex with his soon-to-be wife—and winced. "Not exactly."

"Head-banging music?"

Gray laughed. "At times, yes. Look, San Francisco's special to us. I'd like to get married there now and then we can do another ceremony later if she wants to. Whatever she wants."

"Are you hoping to use the church?"

"No. Do you happen to have some grounds nearby maybe? I want to make it easy on you, but I realize holding it in the house of the Lord might be a bit much for...reasons." Gray took another quick glance inside the restaurant and noticed Jazz had toed off her flip flops and had curled her bare legs under herself on the seat. "Plus, I'm pretty sure she's going to want to be barefoot. It's her thing."

Father Freeley chuckled. "I can do you one better than the church itself. We're right next door to a park with numerous hills. On a clear day, and from the right vantage spot, you can see the bridge in the distance."

"The Golden Gate?"

"Is there any other?"

"No. Not really." Gray grinned. "Does this mean you're saying you'll do it? You'll marry us? Please. I promise, after this one lapse of premarital sex we'll be good Catholics from here on out." One lapse plus about ten thousand. But his fingers of his free hand were crossed in his pocket, so the fib didn't count.

"Twist my robe, why don't you? Of course I will. I would never stand in the path of true love. But one request." He lowered his voice to a near-whisper. "Can you sign a T-shirt for me? I have a teenage niece who would love some memorabilia from a head-banging band."

"Sure thing. Thank you so much."

They finalized a few details then Gray hung up and hurriedly called Lila. "Tell me you're coming tomorrow."

"Well, hello to you too," she said drily. "Yes, I'm coming. Though next time, I'd appreciate some notice to do damage control. You do realize the paparazzi will probably get their hands on this info? Thanks to you, I have no time to work my spin."

"The spin is I want to marry my girl, hopefully quickly and privately enough that no one with a telephoto lens will find out."

"Dream on, rockstar."

"You're the second person to say that to me today." Shaking it off, he waved to Jazz through the glass and held up his finger to indicate one more minute when she frowned. Time was running out. "Look, I need a favor."

"A favor other than interrupting my work in the middle of the week to drive up to San Francisco?"

"You're not driving. You're taking your husband's private jet and bringing the band with you."

"How did you know?"

"Lucky guess. Plus I couldn't imagine you sitting in a smog-filled car for five hours." He grinned. "I need a T-shirt."

"Then how are you affording a wedding?"

He had to laugh. "We're doing it pretty low-key. Though, shit, she needs a dress. Can you find one for her?" He relayed a few more details about the church and the park next door, waiting while she wrote down the address. "Oh, and make sure Harper comes. No matter what, Harper needs to be there."

"Anything else? My personal assistant will just be so bored if you don't keep giving me tasks to pass on to her."

"About the T-shirt." He explained about Father Freeley, then blew out a breath. He hadn't talked as much in the last month as he had in the last ten minutes. "Do we have anything left merchwise?"

"We're in the process of coordinating new merchandise for the album and tour. The numerous delays on said album led to the merchandise being delayed also. We're expecting a shipment next week."

"Next week is too late. C'mon, one damn shirt?"

"The only thing we have left in house is the shirts for Simon's Skanks."

He chuckled. "Simon's Sirens? That'll do."

"No, I'd swear it says skanks."

Knowing Lila's sense of humor could be sarcastic on the best day, he just went with it. "Okay, fine. Bring one, please."

"Surely there's more. Do you need flowers for her hair?"

"Fuck. I didn't even think of flowers. Are they necessary?"

"In a wedding? Of course not. Neither are the wedding bands—" At his groan, she sighed. "Seriously, Grayson, have you not done one thing in preparation?"

"At least we have our marriage license. We got it as soon as I got back from rehab in case we carved out time for the wedding before the tour."

"One thing taken care of. I'm so proud."

"There's one more. I also rented the penthouse suite at the Palatial in San Fran. They bled me dry for two nights. And I think they gave me a discount when I told them my name."

"Right, of course you'd get the place for the honeymoon squared away. Because that benefits you. All you men are the same." It sounded like Lila thumped something in the background. "Where is the love? Where is the romance?"

"Can you bring some of that too? I have the love part down, I think." He smiled at her disgusted huff. "Cool your jets. I have the wedding bands taken care of. I just, uh, haven't picked them up from the jeweler yet."

"You're kidding me."

"Alas, no. Can you grab those too on the way here?" Before she could say no, he rattled off the jeweler's name and address.

"Your thin ice is about to cave in, pal."

"Thank you. I appreciate it more than I can say." Noticing that Jazz was getting restless—her plate of food was empty, and that was one of the few things that could hold her attention for long these days—he reached for the door handle. "I'll sign anything you want and do two extended solos at every show on the first leg of the tour."

"And an extended solo in the encore. And maybe a book signing."

"For what book?"

"We'll talk later. Ciao." Lila clicked off.

Clearly, he'd just signed his soul away to the devil. Except this one hid her horns beneath layers of perfect blond hair.

"Who was that?" Jazz asked.

"Lila." He pocketed his phone but kept his crossed fingers firmly tucked in his pocket. More lies were coming, and they were basically against the tenets he'd agreed to in rehab. Lies for a good reason were still lies, and he didn't want to start down that path again if he didn't have to.

Unfortunately, right now he had no choice.

"Why did you call her?"

"She needs me back in the studio again."

"What? Why? Your parts were all set. I heard them. They were incredible. Jimmy Page couldn't have done better."

He slid into the booth and leaned across the table to cup her cheeks in her hands. "Keep talking like that and we'll never get to San Jose."

"Sure, we will. They have rest stops. Besides, I thought ahead for easier access." She slipped something red out of her pocket and pressed it into his hand, right above her plate of demolished chicken. Seriously, he wasn't even sure she'd left the bones.

Then he refocused on what she'd handed him. Lacy. Tiny. Damp.

"Holy fu—nballs."

She only smirked. "When he's born, you can go back to using the word every five minutes. I may even let you have an extended session saying the word in my ear while you demonstrate a live action sequence."

"You *may* let me?" He tucked the pair of panties into his pocket, barely resisting the urge to sniff them. Hell, if there hadn't been grandparents with some young kids in the next booth, he would've buried his face in them.

"There is no may, Yoda. There is only do."

"Someone's mood has improved." He picked up one discarded breast from her plate. "That chicken tasted good going down, huh?"

"Not all that tasted good going down." She smacked her lips and slid out of the booth to slip back into her shoes, mischief dancing in her eyes.

He chuckled. "You're a dirty bird."

"Duh." She dumped out her tray in the garbage and returned to tug him out of the booth. "Well, c'mon then. If we have to get right back so you can head into the studio, we have to get to Molly's in a hurry. No more sidetrips."

"Tell your belly that," he said, following her out to the parking lot. Watching her ass sway unabashedly the whole time.

"Your son is offended by that comment." She got into the passenger side of the car and turned on the radio as soon as he started the ignition. An Oblivion song was playing—their first big hit, "The Becoming." The song that he'd written with

Deacon that had led to him and Jazz being invited to join the band.

He smiled at her across the small space that separated them. Even that felt like too much. "We've come a long way, haven't we?"

"Yeah." Her smile was wistful. "It hasn't been all that long since we joined the band, but God, everything has changed."

"Not quite a year yet. One hell of an anniversary." He brushed her hair out of her face and rubbed his thumb over her full lower lip. "Dylan Edward Duffy."

She blinked. "What?"

"The kid's name. What do you think?"

"I—I don't know. We haven't even begun to think of names. I'm only on the Bs in my baby name book."

He reversed then drove to the exit. "Let it sit. See what you think."

"Edward for a middle name?"

"Unless you want to make it Edwards."

"That sounds so stuffy. Like he should be in Parliament or something."

"Wrong country, but President would be cool." He shot her a grin as he headed toward the entrance to the freeway. "Better than a rock star."

"What's so bad about being a rock star? It lets me bang lots of dudes." Pursing her lips, she slid him a glance. "So, um, about those Raiders."

It felt so good to laugh as he reached out to toy with her hair. Someday he might not need to touch her every minute, but that day wasn't coming anytime soon. "The only dude you're banging for the rest of your life is me. Deal with it, Duffy."

It took her a second to realize what he'd said, but when she did, a slow smile dawned across her face. "I like the sound of that."

He did too, a hell of a lot. And hopefully by this time tomorrow, it would be official.

If he didn't colossally fuck up the biggest day of his life.

CHAPTER FIVE

The address on the piece of paper turned out to be in a crappy neighborhood filled with crammed together row houses and cans of overflowing garbage serving as curb appeal. Jazz had even seen a toilet in front of one house, sitting in the middle of the lawn and filled with blooming flowers as if it were some kind of urn.

"Nice digs your sister has," Gray said, peering through the windshield as they crept along the street, searching for the right house number.

"Is there a college around here? These look like frat houses. See that dude sitting on the hood of his car over there? He has a keg next to the tire."

"Guys in frats aren't the only ones who drink from kegs."

"I know that. I'm just saying. It has a young vibe."

"Not the only kind of vibe it has," he muttered. "What's the number again?"

She read it to him while trying not to smear the ink on the page from her damp fingers. The nerves were back, and this time they'd brought their friends goose bumps and slight nausea. She seriously hoped the morning sickness had not decided to make another reappearance now. It was heading toward night, for one thing, and for another, throwing up upon meeting someone wasn't exactly the way to make a killer first impression.

Biting her lip, she scanned the houses out the window. "Did we pack crackers, by any chance?"

"I didn't. Did you?"

"If I knew that, would I be asking?"

"The chicken afterglow has clearly worn off. There—that's the one we're looking for." He pulled the car over and glanced at her, apparently noticing her distress. "We passed a convenience store a few blocks ago. After we meet Molly, you can stay here and visit and I'll go see if I can find you something to settle your stomach."

"Don't forget the Pepto."

He grabbed her hand and brushed his lips over her knuckles. "She's going to love you. It's impossible not to." When she didn't respond, he added, "I'd be thrilled if you were my sister."

"Sicko. I already sort of was. And you see how *that* turned out." Pointedly, she looked down at her belly and he laughed.

They got out and stood on the curb, staring at the multi-family house in front of them. Sunset wasn't too far away and the rundown brown building in front of them didn't look any better in the soft pink and gold haze of almost-twilight. "So, I guess we should go see if she lives upstairs or down." She frowned. "Oh shit, I was supposed to call and let her know when we were close."

"Call her now. She didn't say how close, right?"

She rolled her eyes and started heading up the sidewalk. "Good thing you're hot, because you're a total pain in the ass."

"Hello, Dylan is listening. I am offended on his behalf."

Ignoring him, she jogged up the crumbling steps and stopped in front of the row of mailboxes. Three of them. Box number two was for the second floor and was labeled Molly McIntire, written in fading purple ink covered by a piece of peeling tape.

Jazz's already iffy belly sank down to her toes and roiled. Molly's name was the only one on the mailbox, not their mother's.

And sticking out of the top of the mailbox was an eviction notice.

"Nice decorating scheme," Gray said, stopping beside her and gesturing to the weathered gnome holding a daisy that was guarding the front door.

Saying nothing, she pulled out the eviction notice and pressed it into his hand.

He read it silently, his gaze lifting to hers. "Guess it's a good thing we got here before she got booted." His brows knitted. "Unless that's why she contacted you in the first place."

"God, now you sound like Harper."

Moving past her, he aimed for the second door and knocked. When he didn't get a response, he pulled it open, revealing a narrow hallway and a flight of stairs to the left. To the right was the door for apartment number three.

Gray glanced back and motioned her forward. "After you."

Jazz bit her lip and dragged her attention away from the window covered with bars that she'd just noticed. That was probably some sort of design. Most likely the bars weren't for protection.

She hoped.

She went inside and started to lead the way up the stairs, but he took her arm and gently nudged her behind him. "Nope. No can do. Until we see what's on the other side of that door, you're riding shotgun. Sorry."

Her feminist side demanded she argue. Her newly emerging mom side, however, had no problem letting him check the situation out first, even if that made her a wuss.

A nauseous wuss to boot.

She nodded and he ascended the stairs, still holding the eviction notice. He knocked once, twice, three times. Finally on the fourth, a guy bellowed, "Who the fuck is it?"

Gray raised a brow in Jazz's direction. "Don't think that's the welcome wagon." He turned toward the door. "Avon. Sale on lip gloss. Interested?"

"Jesus, G." Jazz shoved him aside and knocked politely. "Hi, this is Jazz—Jasmine Edwards. I'm looking for Molly?"

"Hang on."

"What'd I say about behind me?" Gray grabbed her shoulders and eased her behind him, so that her ass was pressed against the wobbly railing. "If this looks as dicey as it sounds, we're outta here," he added in an undertone. "Sister or not."

Reluctantly, Jazz nodded, though she had no such intention of fleeing so soon. Now that she'd come all this way, she needed to see Molly. Needed to listen to her talk and watch her smile and hopefully, hug the stuffing out of her. She couldn't just turn her back without making a real attempt.

Maybe the guy was just the growly sort but was a perfectly decent human being.

The door swung open and a guy with a purple faux hawk leaned out, his gut preceding him. He wore disturbingly tight jeans, some kind of spiked belt and had a large tattoo of the devil—who happened to be frothing at the mouth—on his right pec. "You callin' yourself Jasmine?" he demanded, staring hard at Gray. "It fits."

Not rising to the bait, Gray jerked his thumb over his shoulder at Jazz. "That's Jasmine. I'm her husband. Where is Molly?"

"Husband? Since when?" A tall girl in a bra and booty shorts shoved past past the smirker in the doorway and dragged a mile of honey-blond curls out of her face. "I thought you were—" She broke off as her eyes locked with Jazz's.

Jazz opened her mouth, intending to say something. Anything. *Hello. How are you? I'm sorry I forgot to call back.*

But a wave of nausea strangled anything but a choked, "Move!" She cupped her hand over her mouth and shoved her way into the apartment, frantically looking right and left over piles of debris that resembled furniture until she noticed a door on the opposite side of the living room/kitchen combo. She barreled into it and slammed the door shut before losing her well-earned chicken and half of her esophagus in the toilet.

Fifteen minutes later, she emerged from the bathroom. Everyone—minus Gray who lurked outside the bathroom like a sentinel—was still in the doorway of the apartment. Apartment was kind of a compliment, since it resembled a large coat closet more than an actual living area. And its inhabitants were now staring at Jazz as if she were an alien life form.

"Are you okay?" Gray asked, reaching for her.

Jazz lifted her damp hair away from her cheeks. Washing her face and rinsing out her mouth twenty times had helped revive her, but only marginally. "I'm fine."

"Dude, are you knocked up?" Faux hawk asked.

Gray pressed his mouth against Jazz's ear. "We can still leave. Just walk out the door and keep going."

"Yes, I'm pregnant."

Molly frowned in the general direction of Jazz's belly. "Where is it?"

For unknown reasons, Jazz glanced down at her stomach too. She knew her bump wouldn't be any bigger than it had been at the doctor's office, and hell, she had photographic proof in her purse that she had a kid in there. But a strange panic seized her and she cupped her belly, wavering a little on her feet.

"Easy." Gray guided her to the nearest seat, a recliner that had clearly seen better days. "Can she have some water? Or something that isn't toxic?"

"Shush," Jazz mumbled, sagging into his side as he sat on the arm of the chair. She tried not to look around at the mess—the piles of discarded newspapers and takeout cartons, the empty beer bottles that littered the tables, the dust that seemed to cover every surface—but it was almost impossible.

Jazz wrinkled her nose. Equally impossible to ignore was the faint stench of pot that hung in the air.

Molly headed into the galley-style kitchen and pulled down a glass from the cupboard. She filled it with tap water then crossed the room and handed it to Jazz, moving back quickly before their fingers could touch. "I didn't know you were pregnant."

Jazz sipped the lukewarm water and gripped the glass to give her hands something to do. "We haven't really made it public yet.

Our manager likes to spin things a certain way so she picks the timing for most announcements."

"Even your baby? Wow, that's wack." Molly sat on the edge of the coffee table and let her arms dangle between her legs as she looked from Jazz to Gray. Jazz was sure that the fact that her sister's current pose nearly made her extremely ample breasts fall out of her bra was just a coincidence.

As way the wolfish way she was now eyeing Gray and licking her lips. Literally.

"So y'all are married? When did that happen?"

"It hasn't yet."

"But he said he was your husband. Or is that common law?" Molly decided to change positions, this time relaxing with her hands behind her on the coffee table, therefore pushing her breasts in the air.

"Do you think you could put a shirt on?" Jazz asked, not for Gray's benefit but her own. Gray hadn't spared Molly more than a look so far.

"Why? If I wasn't meant to show these babies off, God wouldn't have been so generous with them." Molly laughed and hopped up off the coffee table. "Hey Junior. Grab my shirt off the bed, would you?"

Like the dutiful whatever-the-hell he was, faux hawk abandoned his post in the doorway to go retrieve Molly's shirt from an adjacent room that was presumably the bedroom.

"Junior, huh? So he's not the first formed in that mold?" Gray kicked out his long legs and crossed them. "So glad to hear that."

Molly narrowed her eyes. "You makin' fun of my boyfriend? He's in a band, same as you." She crossed her arms over God's generous gifts. "Matter of fact, we're *both* in a band."

"Where's our mother?" Jazz demanded, filing away the band information for later. Way later, when her head stopped exploding from the barrage of new data.

"Mol, here."

Molly caught the shirt Junior tossed her and pulled it on. And oh, what a shirt it was. It appeared to be made out of some kind of lime green mesh and showed off almost as much skin when she was wearing it as without. She turned back to face Jazz and Gray, propping her hands on her equally generous hips.

Whereas Jazz was stacked up top and nowhere else, Molly had been the recipient of a trifecta of presents from the body fairy—huge boobs, curvy butt and long legs that could make a tree feel jealous. The tiny waist, huge blue eyes and shampoo commercial-shiny curls were bonuses.

"My mother isn't here."

"Your mother," Jazz repeated, saying the words again to lessen their sting. But it wasn't the repetition of them that accomplished that. It was the strong arm around her shoulders that offered her a place to lean even when she couldn't admit that she needed to.

"Yeah, so what? I'm grown. I don't need anyone taking care of me."

"Right. Seventeen is grown. And you're not even seventeen yet."

Molly's mouth curved in something awfully close to a sneer. "You're not that much older than me and you're some kind of married and knocked up."

"I'm plenty older than you and I've also been the next thing to on my own since—"

"Since you were fourteen, yeah, yeah. I read your press bio. Until you moved in with this one's family," she pointed at Gray, "and scored yourself a rich man. But not all of us care about money and status."

Gray glanced around the apartment. "Yeah, I'd say that's obvious."

"Who says we ain't got money or status?" Junior dropped down on the coffee table and Jazz wondered how it didn't break in half from his considerable bulk. "Just because we choose to live here doesn't mean—"

"You're living with your boyfriend at the age of sixteen?" Jazz interrupted. "And Mom's just gone?"

Gray tugged the folded eviction notice out of his pocket. "Speaking of choosing to live places, I think your fortunate run here is almost up."

Molly snatched the paper out of Gray's hand. "He doesn't live here," she said, obviously distracted as she read the paper she held.

"Hell I don't." Junior pounded a meaty fist on the coffee table. "I cook, I clean, I take care of this place while you go out whoring around."

"Wait a second," Jazz and Gray said simultaneously.

But Molly didn't need their help.

She turned toward Junior and lifted a brow. "Did you just call me a whore?"

Junior set his jaw. "And if I did? Then what? You gonna kick me out before you're kicked to the curb yourself?"

Without hesitation, she pointed to the door. "Get the hell out."

For a long moment, tension throbbed in the room like a heartbeat. Jazz felt Gray brace beside her and knew he wouldn't hesitate to leap to defend a girl who hadn't been kind to either of them.

She'd never loved him more.

"You know what?" Junior hauled himself up and stalked toward the bedroom. "I don't need this. I'm outta here."

Less than a minute later, him and a raggedy duffel bag of his stuff were gone.

Molly cupped her elbows and stared at the closed door, still vibrating in its hinges. For the first time since they'd arrived, she looked less than sure of herself. She actually looked...desolate.

Jazz glanced at Gray, who was already looking at her. Then he sighed and stood. "Do you have any place to stay?"

Jazz gripped the arms of the chair. She'd known he would make some sort of effort to ease Molly's discomfort—as would she once the numbness that had descended over her wore off—but even she hadn't expected *that*. There were kind gestures, and there was going above and beyond.

"Yeah." Molly stuffed her hands in her back pockets. "Right here."

"I think that eviction notice says otherwise. Do you have a way to pay?"

"I've got it covered." Molly smirked at him, but her eyes were as heavy and dark as bruises. "Don't worry about it, moneybags. Y'all can just head on back to your fancy house up in LA now."

Idly, Gray stroked Jazz's hair. "Babe, why don't you take the car and go down the street to that convenience store we passed on the way in? Get those crackers we talked about." While he spoke, he never took his eyes off Molly.

Jazz pressed her fist against her growling stomach. At the moment, crackers sounded like a gourmet meal. But why was he sending her off? "What's going on?"

"Nothing. Just go get your crackers and come back." He dangled the keys in front of her and she took them, too tired to argue. Besides, she knew he wouldn't do anything to harm her in any way. It wasn't like her relationship with her sister could be damaged more.

They didn't have one.

When she didn't move, he leaned down and brushed a kiss over her forehead. "Fifteen minutes," he said, and somehow those words were a promise.

Let me take care of this for you.

She didn't know what that meant, but she trusted him enough to not make an issue of it.

Nodding, she rose and headed to the door. Then she turned back to look at the girl who didn't resemble her at all, in any way. "I was told several times that coming here was a mistake, but I didn't want to believe it. Because I only have one sister, and it seemed like a gift that I might get her back."

Something flickered in Molly's eyes, though she remained silent.

"You might prove me wrong this time, but I won't let you change me for the next. And maybe that's the biggest gift I can ask for." Jazz exchanged a glance with Gray before walking out and closing the door behind her.

After he heard Jazz's footsteps descend down the stairs outside Molly's apartment, Gray sat in the chair she had vacated and tugged out his wallet. He wasn't at all sure this was the best move to make, but he was running out of time—and options. "So what will it take?"

Molly stopped staring off into space and shot him a look dripping with derision. "What will what take?"

"Tomorrow needs to be special for Jazz and I'm willing to make sure of that through any means necessary. I think she'd be happy to have you there, and I'm gonna guess that you aren't real interested in doing anything to make her happy. But you do need this." He inclined his chin at his wallet. "So...let's talk. Fast. Before she comes back."

"You're paying me off?" Shock coated Molly's previously husky voice. "For what?"

"I just told you, she needs you there tomorrow. And I need her to be happy." At Molly's blank look, he realized he was skipping steps in his haste to get this squared away.

If Lila thought he was lacking preparedness for the wedding, he could just imagine what she would have to say about his methods here.

"We're getting married tomorrow. I hope. It's a surprise. A *surprise*," he repeated. "Which means if you blab to her, you're going to answer to me."

"Getting married because she's got the bun in the oven, I'm guessing." Molly's smirk was back in full force as she sat on the back of the loveseat and propped her bare feet on the cushions. Evidently she and her former "boyfriend" didn't like actually sitting on the parts of furniture actually intended for that purpose.

"No, getting married because we love each other and we want to be together."

"You already are together." She used the back of the loveseat like a slide and bounced onto the cushions, a rather impressive feat considering how tall she was. "Unless you're trying to lock her down because of that whole love triangle business."

"So you've heard of that but you hadn't heard the gossip about us being engaged or her being pregnant. You have selective hearing."

"I think you do too. How do you even know that kid's yours?"

He didn't let the jab take root, because it was baseless and he knew it. "How do I know you're even really her sister?"

Molly pursed her lips in an expression surprisingly similar to Jazz's. It was the first time he'd seen any sort of resemblance between them, and the glimpse startled him into sitting back in the chair while she rose to rifle through a file cabinet that was being used for an end table. She dug out a sheaf of papers and strode over to him, thrusting one out. "That's my birth certificate. Mama left it with the other papers when she took off."

Rather than looking at the paper, he looked at her instead. "How long have you been on your own?"

Immediately the defensiveness snapped back into place. "Why does it matter?"

He sat back in the chair and glanced out the curtainless window. Bars crisscrossed across it, blocking out a lot of the light. "My family took in foster kids from the time I was small. I saw a lot of them come and go. I heard a lot of stories."

She gripped her elbows and looked anywhere but at him. "Hearing isn't the same as living it."

"No. You're right. But I lived it with Jazz. I'll spend the rest of my life trying to make up for those years she spent afraid and alone. You deserve that too."

He didn't expect her bitter laughter or the single tear that tracked down her cheek. She swiped it away angrily. "Not everyone gets a fairy tale like she has. Most kids don't hook up with some rich dude in their foster family. They don't join bands and achieve what she has already."

"That should give you hope."

"Hope? What the fuck is that?" She kicked at the wicker basket of magazines and assorted crap and sent it falling on its side. "That's what they sell on your side of town, not mine."

"If you think she won't want you on our side of town, you're nuts."

Her chin came up. "Oh really? She seemed pretty dismissive when she walked out the door. Not that hard to push her away, just like someone else I used to know."

"Why would you write to someone, claim you want to meet, then try to push her away?" He stared at the paper in his hand without seeing the print. "You intended to take advantage of her," he said quietly. "What made you change your mind?" When she didn't respond, he took a guess. "Because she's pregnant?"

Her face softened, answering the question for him. He nodded. "So the girl without hope still has a heart."

"Fuck you. You don't know a thing about me."

"I know she's been through as much as you, and no one would love you more, if you only let her. You loved her once. She told me you called her Mine."

Molly let out another of those rasping laughs that sounded as if they were torn from her throat. "I loved my mother too. What'd that get me?"

"The same thing it got her. She did it anyway."

"We aren't the same. Not even close." She snapped a hairband off her wrist and tied up her curls with a few jerky flicks of her fingers. "You don't see me setting up house with a druggie either."

The dig hit its mark, as intended. Mainly because any reminder of how far he'd let himself sink—and all that he'd almost lost—always hollowed him out. "I'm clean now."

"Sure you are."

"I'd be happy to take a drug test." He sniffed. The scent of marijuana still stung the air. "How about you, kiddo?"

"I'm not a kiddo. And what's wrong with a little pot? It's no worse than alcohol."

"Right. I told myself that too about pot. Then about coke. Then I found myself in rehab."

"That's on you. Some of us have better control of ourselves."

"Some of us also have people we want to be better for. Do you have one of those too?" She didn't speak. "No? Didn't think so. I did. She's the reason I'm sitting here right now with nothing in my veins but blood. She's the reason I came here even though I didn't want to. Even though I suspected you were going to use her kind heart against her. Apples and trees, you know?"

"Your perfect angel is from the same fucking tree."

"Yeah, she is. Maybe you could try remembering that the next time you think you can use her to make a few quick bucks." He leaned forward. "I'm curious. How'd you intend to do it? Cozy up to her then rob her blind someday when she let her guard down? Maybe sell stories about her private life to the tabloids?"

"You're goddamn suspicious for someone who's sucked on a silver spoon since birth."

"The only spoon I'm sucking nowadays is my own. Can you say the same?" He gestured around the apartment. "Did you get this on your own or did you do whatever necessary to get the money you needed?"

She glared at him out of slitted eyes. "How dare you."

"Oh, I dare. And I don't judge." He lifted his hands. "But your sister isn't going to be your next meal ticket, you can bet your ass on that." He waited a beat until she stopped pacing long enough to hear him. "Me, on the other hand..."

Her jaw locked. "What the hell's that supposed to mean?"

"It means I'll pay for what I want."

"Sure, you will. That's how guys you like operate. Everything's about cash."

"Isn't it?"

"You sure your precious wifey would be onboard with these tactics of yours?" She stopped her restless movements and clamped her arms over her chest. "I'm not so sure."

"You have no idea what she would or wouldn't be onboard with until you get to know her. But hey, your choice. I'm not about to plead your case. You want the truth?"

She spared him a brief look. "Your version, you mean?"

"Yeah. You showing up now is damn inconvenient for me. See, we've gone through a hell of a lot of shit to get to this place. And then you write her a letter with your little sob story and she's right back in the pit she climbed out of. I want you gone." He lifted his wallet. "I'm willing to pay you to make you stay that way. If you come with us tonight and go to the ceremony tomorrow, I'll make it worth your while to leave us alone for good."

He was totally bluffing. He didn't have that kind of money, and if he did, he wouldn't blow it on paying off a teenager with a probably well-earned chip on her shoulder. Jazz and his kid came first, always, which meant the money he earned went to their future. Doing this was a huge gamble. It might end up being worth it or it might screw up what he had with Jazz.

As far as he could tell, he didn't have a lot of options. If he could do something to make his girl happy, he had to try.

"You're paying me off to leave my sister alone," she said, clearly disbelieving. "You want me to be part of this little family day thing and then that's it."

"That about sums it up, yes. And you don't have a lot of time to think about it. Either you say yes now or the deal's off."

"I could tell her what you tried to do. That'd tarnish the fairy tale some, wouldn't it?"

He braced the ankle of one leg on the other, casual as could be. "You could," he said easily. "You want to ruin her wedding day, be my guest."

"Why should I give a shit?" She shoved at a pile of junk on the loveseat and sat in the corner, drawing her legs up to her chest just like Jazz always did.

Curling into themselves to make themselves as small as possible.

"Why do you?" he countered softly. "Except for the fact that the baby she's carrying is your nephew, and it seems to me like you don't have enough family to be turning any away."

She gritted her teeth. "You're giving them to me for one day, then I'm exiled anyway."

"One day's more than you've had for a long time, I'm guessing. And you'll be handsomely paid for your time."

"Rich fucking bastard," she said under her breath, examining her chipped black and blue nail polish. "Fine. Whatever. But my time doesn't come cheap."

"I'm sure." He nearly smiled before took advantage of her distraction to slip the birth certificate in his pocket. He'd be getting that verified before he turned over one dime to her—not that he intended to give her much. If he even had to give her anything at all.

Jazz didn't have much time to work her magic on her sister, but he had faith that she'd pull it out like she always did. She was impossible not to love, and he was willing to bet that would hold true for Molly as well, despite how resistant she was to the idea of family.

"All I have to do is play the part of the happy sister, then I get paid and get gone." She fixated on her feet. "Right?"

"Right. Maybe throw some rice around and pose for a picture or two with the band."

She perked up. "The band? They'll be there?"

"They're supposed to be, yes."

"Nick's hot," she said, her mouth curling in a knowing smile. "Guess Mine thought so too."

"Feel free to ask her. Since, you know, she's wearing my ring." He rose and stuck out a hand to her. "So do we have a deal or not?"

She stared at his hand for a long moment before clasping it and giving it a lackluster pump. "Yeah. Fine. Whatever."

"Oh, and Mol? You just slipped up and called her Mine." He smiled as he heard footsteps on the stairs outside the door. "Better be careful or you might forget you hate her."

"Don't bet on it."

His smile grew as the door swung open. "I'm betting on her," he said, meeting Jazz's gaze. "As I always do."

CHAPTER SIX

Something was afoot.

"Explain to me why she's coming with us again?" Jazz asked as they waited in the parking lot of the gas station while Molly ran inside to get a Slurpee and "something edible." "I expected you to herd me out of there the minute I got back from the store, and instead we're roadtripping."

"We're just taking a detour to San Fran for the night."

Jazz stared hard at the side of Gray's face. He wasn't making eye contact with her, and she knew him well enough to know that meant he was being shifty. Or trying to be. "I thought you had to get back to the studio."

"Yeah, but not until day after tomorrow." He toyed with his iPhone, shuffling through songs. "I thought we'd take a day to—hey," he said as she closed her hand over his.

She got right in his face, nose to nose. "What aren't you telling me?"

He gave her his most innocent look. If she wasn't mistaken, the jerk even batted his ridiculously long lashes at her. "I don't know what you mean, sweetie."

"Don't *sweetie* me. I know when I'm being snowed." She slumped back in her seat and crossed her legs and arms like the pouty teenager she currently felt like.

He knew how she felt about surprises. They made her nervous under the best of circumstances. It had taken years for Christmas to cause her more excitement than anxiety. Too many years of waking up to find nothing under the tree—or worse, some salacious gift from her mama's current boyfriend du jour—had made her dread a time of year that other kids anticipated. Regular surprises weren't much better. In spite of trusting him wholeheartedly, she couldn't help her natural reservations and panic at being kept in the dark. He understood that, or at least she thought he did.

So that must mean that he believed whatever he was up to was worth her momentary discomfort.

"It doesn't snow in California, baby."

She glared at him, but he only laughed.

"Where exactly do you plan for us to stay tonight?"

"All taken care of."

"Mmm-hmm. Are we sharing a room with Molly? Because, hello, awkward."

"Trust me," he said, reaching out to cluck her chin in a way that made her hiss. He just laughed again.

Molly emerged from the gas station and climbed in the backseat, a drink in one hand and a truly awe-inspiring amount of junk food exploding out of the bag she clutched in her other. Noticing Jazz's longing glance, she stuck her drink in the cup holder and fished around in the bag, producing a bag of Skittles. "You still like these?"

"Gimme." Jazz snatched them out of her hand and tore into the bag with gusto. "Thank Jesus," she said in between stuffing her mouth. "He's been trying to starve me."

"Sure I have. How much did they say you weighed this morning at the doctor's again?"

Jazz stopped chowing down long enough to whack his arm. "Shut up. I don't hear you complaining about my boobs."

"God himself wouldn't complain about your boobs."

Molly flopped back in the seat and sucked on her drink. "Seriously, you two are gross."

"You can talk. You answered your door in just a bra."

"But it was a classy bra."

"Sure it was." Jazz set her Skittles on the dashboard. "Christ, now I have to pee. Be right back."

The last thing she heard as she climbed out of the car was Molly. "Pregnancy is totally lame."

Rather than annoying her, it made her grin as she jogged into the gas station and aimed for the bathroom.

The bathroom itself killed her grin right quick, but she made do. She was at the sink washing her hands when her phone rang. After drying off quickly, she tugged it out and smiled at the readout. "Hey you," she said to Harper.

"Hiya. You sound happy."

"I am. Very." She wasn't even sure why. Her nerves about Gray's odd behavior created a low hum under her skin, and she definitely wasn't sure what to make of the whole Molly situation, but for this very moment, she had a family. Her best friend on the phone, a sister, an almost-husband, a baby on the way. She'd never had this much before.

"Oh thank God." Harper let out a long sigh. "It was killing me keeping it in, but I didn't know if he'd tell you right before or what. I figured he'd cave, because who keeps that kind of secret until right before the ceremony?"

Jazz frowned at her reflection in the water-spotted mirror. "What are you talking about?"

Harper didn't speak.

"Hello?"

"Harper is unavailable right now. Call back never," Harper said in a small voice.

Jazz fought a grin. "Harp, you better start talking or I'm going to kick your ass."

"You can't. I'm pregnant," she said after a moment. "*You're* pregnant."

"I so can kick your ass, pregnant or not. I'm little but I'm mighty." As Harper's earlier words finally sank in, she gasped. "Ceremony? Did you say ceremony?"

"No. I absolutely did not." A loud hissing noise filled the line. "Wow, did you hear that? Must be interference." More hissing that sounded suspiciously like someone blowing air. "Sorry, can't hear you! Gotta go."

"Harper McCoy, if you hang up this phone, we're no longer best friends."

The hissing stopped. "Liar."

"I so am." Jazz eased a hip up on the sink, then remembered she was in a gas station bathroom and hopped back off. Ick. "Okay, spill. I won't tell you told me. Promise."

"Aw, dammit, I'm ruining the surprise."

"No, you aren't. You're enhancing the surprise because I fuck—frigging hate surprises and he freaking knows it."

"That's why he's trying to give you a good one and I just screwed it up."

"Well, finish it off. What's going on, dammit?" Jazz demanded.

"Oh fine. I guess there is a sister code. But if you so much as hint that I told you..."

"I would never." Jazz crossed her heart even though there was no one there to witness it. Someone pounded on the bathroom door and she turned the phone against her shoulder. "Just one sec. Sorry." She pressed the phone back to her ear. "Hurry up. I'm in a gas station bathroom."

"Okay, okay, but this is under extreme duress I'm divulging this information."

"Noted. Come on already."

"Gray's planning a big...baby-blessing ceremony in San Fran for you tomorrow. Yes, that's it. It's a big thing now, to bless mother-to-be's bellies. I think he saw it on the Today show. Kind of woo-woo, but hey, you know, whatever flips your crank."

Jazz narrowed her eyes. "You are so full of crap I can smell you from here."

"It's not me you can smell," Harp said, making her laugh in spite of herself. "Oh, look at that. The big guy's ready to go. We have to buy—uh, I have to buy a new dress for tomorrow's baby-blessing."

The puzzle pieces were starting to fit together. Jazz swallowed hard and gripped her phone. "You're coming too?"

"Of course I am. The whole band will be there. For all baby blessings, it's important to have someone you trust at your side to be your witness. In your case, you're getting a bunch of witnesses."

"Oh God. I can't breathe. I need to sit down."

"No, you don't. You need to walk out of the bathroom, head straight for the snack aisle and buy yourself a package of ceremonial cupcakes. The kind with filling that oozes out."

"Okay. Going." Jazz nodded and exited the bathroom, waving in apology at the older lady who waited outside. Ceremonial cupcakes sounded good. So what if she had Skittles in the car? She'd been so good lately, and oh my Lord, she was pretty sure she was getting married tomorrow and she needed a goddamn cupcake.

"Do you have them?" Harper whispered conspiratorially a moment later.

"I can't find them. I think they're out."

"Don't give up so easily. When you find them, I want you to go back to the car and tell Gray you can't wait to have cake tomorrow. Lots and lots of cake."

Jazz frowned at the selection of pastries and baked goods. There wasn't a gooey cream-filled cupcake in sight. "Why would I do that if I'm not supposed to know?"

"Because half the fun of knowing about we—baby-blessing ceremonies in advance is using them to your advantage. You totally need to yank Gray's chain, because he shouldn't have kept something big a surprise anyway. I would have told him that myself had I known about it before a few hours ago."

"You're right. He's totally wrong. So, so wrong." She stared hard at the apple pies and promptly burst into tears.

"Oh great. Now I broke her."

Jazz laughed through her tears at Harper's exasperation. "You didn't break me. He's just so stupidly sweet. He drove all the way out here to meet my sister and—"

"Oh my God, I completely forgot the Molly situation. I'm a horrible friend. I got so distracted with online shopping for a decent dress I could pick up super fast at the store that I just zoned out. What happened? Tell me everything."

"It was...interesting. *Is* interesting. She's in the car with us and we're on our way to San Fran." Jazz glanced up and sniffled as she saw Gray's long legs eating up the pavement as he strode toward the store. "Oh fuck, here he comes. I took too long. See you later. I mean, tomorrow. Oh dammit, I'll try to call you tonight. Thank you. Love you. Bye." She clicked off and shoved the phone in her pocket right before Gray spotted her and started weaving his way through the aisles.

She undid her pigtails and let her hair hide her probably blotchy face. Whew. Talk about close.

"What are you doing? You've been gone forever." Once he finally reached her, he glanced down at the bakery section and chuckled. "Should've known you'd wander this—hey, look at me." He brushed her hair back and tipped up her chin. "Are you sick again? Why are you crying?"

One look into his concerned gray eyes and she was done for. The tears started, worse than before. "I just really, really want apple pie," she whispered, hurling herself into his arms.

"Hey, what's the matter? You can have pie. Here. Have a whole bunch of pies." Wrapping one arm around her waist, he guided her back to the display and pushed about six of them into her arms. "You probably shouldn't have them all at once, but one a day should be okay."

Tears streamed down as she stared at the plastic-wrapped pies. "People thought I was nuts for loving you. That you were messed up and wouldn't ever go back to being my Gray. But you always were. They didn't understand."

"You gave me no choice but to get better. You wouldn't allow me not to." He chuckled and kissed the top of her head. "We better get back to the car. Molly might drive off if we don't get moving."

"No one else but you would bring her with us." She tipped up her face, needing to see him even through the blur of her tears. "She treated us like total crap when we got there and you just wanted to make sure I was happy. You always want that, no matter what."

"Yeah, I do." He cleared his throat. "And sometimes I make choices that might not seem like they're the best, but I'd do anything for you—"

She leaned up to silence him with a kiss. "I know."

He probably thought she might be annoyed once she found out about the wedding, because most women wanted to have a say in planning their ceremony. Not her. This was perfect. She didn't care one whit about the shindig itself. She just wanted that shiny band on her finger and for him to be hers. The rest was just details.

"Come on. Let's go pay." He took half her apple pies and she started to tell him to put them back, that she really didn't want them.

Then again, who knew where they were spending the night? Maybe room service would suck. And she did like apple pie.

Shrugging, she followed him up to the checkout. She was getting married tomorrow. She deserved extra freaking dessert.

A roadtrip with his surprisingly cheerful fiancée and snarky sister-in-law hadn't been in the cards two days ago, but it had turned out pretty well.

At least until he learned that the hotel did not have any other open rooms, no matter how much he cajoled or offered money he did not want to spend on things other than oh, mortgage payments, food and child-related costs.

"Sir, I'm very sorry. We're at full occupancy due to several events in town this weekend." The woman behind the desk consulted the ledger in front of her while Molly sighed loudly and Jazz looked around in dazed wonder.

He didn't blame her. The place was seriously lush. Chandeliers dripped glittering crystals and miles of gleaming marble floor stretched as far as the eye could see. Women glided past in pastel dresses that probably cost more than some people made in a year. Even the elevators were bronze, for God's sake.

"You don't have any other options for me?" Taking advantage of Jazz's distraction, he leaned across the desk and lowered his voice. "Look, I booked the penthouse suite so we could, you know, have privacy. Hard to do that with a sixteen-year-old two feet away, snapping her gum."

"Seventeen in two days," Molly informed the hotel employee. "Thank you very much."

"I do have one option for you. We can bring in a cot for the living area. There is a door that locks between the two areas." The woman glanced up and smiled brightly as if she'd just offered him a million dollars. "That should help, no?"

He nearly said "no" but thought better of it. What other alternatives were there? He couldn't let her sleep in the car. Well, he could, though he doubted Jazz would go for it.

"Fine."

"Oh yay. I get to listen to you two screw like minxes all night." Molly rolled her eyes and stalked off to the nearest elevator.

"It's screw like bunnies," Jazz called after her, to which Molly lifted the middle finger, drawing more than a few surprised looks.

Jazz laughed. "She definitely has my temper."

Gray shook his head. While Jazz was in awe over the hotel, he lived in a perpetual state of amazement that Jazz could view Molly's insolence with such good humor. "We'll take the cot," he told the woman behind the desk. "And possibly a gag, if you have it."

"Ooh, kinky." Jazz hipchecked him into a smile in spite of himself.

The concierge didn't blink. "We can supply you with any number of marital aids. If you'd like our list of—"

"No. We're fine. Thanks."

"Says who? Gimme." Jazz leaned forward, her loose hair dangling. "I mean, yes, please, we would love to see this list of available marital aids."

The woman handed over a laminated menu and the room keys. "Enjoy your stay at the Palatial Suites. Please ring the desk if we can assist you in any way."

Jazz snatched the laminated menu—and yeah, he didn't want to imagine why it was *laminated*—and bit her lower lip. "So how do we get a hold of this stuff? Is there room service like with food?"

"Yes, ma'am. Simply request what you would like from the desk."

"Huh. Okay. Thank you." Jazz headed off to the elevator while he made arrangements with the bellhop to carry up their stuff. Not that he and Jazz had a ton of things, but Molly had packed her entire life into four bags. She might've just emptied her closet.

When he joined the ladies in the elevator, he shouldn't have been surprised to see their heads bent together over the menu of sex toys. He shouldn't have been, but he was.

"I shouldn't let you look at this," Jazz said, tugging it away.

"Hell yes, you should. I'm no virgin." Molly dragged it back and cocked her head. "Some of this stuff sounds intriguing."

"Yes, and feel free to learn more about it when you're eighteen." Jazz snatched back the sheet and stuffed it in the back of her jean shorts like a weapon.

"Uh, you don't know where that's been." Gray took it from her and hit the button for the penthouse suite.

He didn't mean to look at the menu. Really he didn't. Why did they need sex toys when her breasts and the sweet heat between her legs were more than enough to entertain him for a lifetime? But as he took in the array of items offered, from ticklers to fur-lined handcuffs to dildos, his mind went wild. It wasn't as if they ever got much time alone, living in the house with the rest of the band. Sex was mostly impromptu and quick. They never got a chance to...play.

He cast a dark look at Molly. She would not stop them tonight. If he had to turn the music up to scream and bar the door between the rooms, he would.

"I think he's decided he's interested," Molly said with a smirk, watching the numbers climb above the door.

The door snicked open and he ushered them out of the elevator and into the suite, registering the "oohs" and "aahs" with a distracted smile. He had a call to make to Lila to finalize a few more arrangements and then he was calling down to the concierge to order about sixteen things off that menu. The bill for this place with the add-ons would probably empty out his bank account but he didn't give a shit.

He'd be responsible again next week.

"Gray, come look at this," Jazz called as he pried out his cell phone and headed into the bedroom. "French doors to the balcony. Oh my God, you can see the Golden Gate."

"Think he's got something else on his mind at the moment," Molly replied.

"Dinner? Yeah, me too. I saw a Chinese place a few blocks over."

"He wants a pussy platter, not Pu Pu, but nice try."

Jazz snorted out a laugh but Gray ignored them both as he sat on the ginormous, silk-sheeted bed. He banked on Jazz staying distracted long enough for him to ascertain everything was on track on Lila's end for tomorrow.

As far as Pu Pu platters and Jazz's stomach, she would have to wait. His schedule for the evening included taking advantage of some of the hotel's amenities. They had a ton of sightseeing to do, and he intended to start with the highlights of her body.

"Eat an apple pie," he advised before he called Lila.

A few minutes later, they ended their abbreviated, hushed phone call and he called down to the front desk. He ordered a few of the things that had caught his eye—and snagged the attention of other parts of his anatomy—and got off the phone just as Jazz bounced onto the mattress.

"Did you just order something called a two-headed monster?" She cocked her head. "I'm guessing that isn't from the Chinese place."

"Two-headed massager, and no, it wasn't." He kicked back on the bed and extended a hand to her. "C'mere."

She crawled up the bed and curled up against him, but he could tell she was more concerned with where Molly was than with a quickie before dinner. Or better yet, a long, slow one. They'd been driving for hours, and he wanted nothing more than to sink into her and savor their last night together before they became official. And then tomorrow night, he'd savor her even more.

Assuming she actually agreed to marry him after she found out the stunt he'd pulled. Both stunts, that is—the secret wedding, and the plan to pay off Molly, in spite of the fact that he was determined that no money would change hands. If Jazz found out what he'd done before Molly came to her senses regarding the importance of having her sister in her life, he might be divorced before he got married.

"I'm going out to explore," Molly called.

Jazz propped her elbow on his chest and leaned half off the bed. "Wait. Where are you going?"

The door to the suite slammed shut.

Jazz shut her eyes and heaved out a breath. "Is this what parenting is going to be like?"

"I doubt it. Our kid won't be perusing menus of sex toys until they're at least fifty."

She giggled. "I shouldn't have let her look at it, but I forgot for a minute she's only seventeen. Hell, not even quite seventeen yet. She acts so much older. Her boyfriend—lover—ick, whatever he was had to be our age." She shuddered.

"She's been on our own for a while. That changes you." He brushed his fingers over her cheek. "I don't know how it didn't change you more. Shows how strong a will you have."

"I'm naïve. Even with everything, I still want to pretend that people aren't always out to con you. That sometimes someone might just want to be your friend or get to know you just because. No ulterior motive." She gazed off in the distance over his shoulder. "This business fucks with your head. Everyone wants their pound of flesh. I guess it's hard for me to understand that now I'm the one someone might want a piece of. I'm used to being the girl with nothing."

"You were never the girl with nothing." He rubbed her lower lip with his thumb. "You have more than anyone I've ever known. Right here." He slid his hand up over the slight swell of her belly to cover her heart.

"You're biased," she said, smiling.

"Damn right. Don't forget stupidly in love too. I'm sure I'm imagining all your countless attributes." Laughing, he pulled her more fully on top of him and cupped her cheeks in his hands, drawing her mouth onto his. "Like the fact that you make the most of every pocket of time you're presented with. Such as right this very instant..."

"Hmm, yeah, alone time isn't something we get a lot of." She glanced down between them. "And with him coming, that won't be improving soon."

"You're absolutely right. So we should take advantage of every opportunity." He flicked her nose. "Get naked."

She grinned and sat back to tug her shirt over her head. The blush pink bra she wore beneath nearly made him weep. "You're bossy."

"You know it."

A knock sounded at the door and he groaned, dipping his head back.

"Is that your special delivery?" she asked, waggling her brows.

"Oh yeah." He nearly toppled her on her side in his haste to get off the bed. "Be right back."

At the door, he met the hotel employee and tipped him in exchange for the plain brown handled bag that was about an inconspicuous as a heart attack. The grin and wink the guy sent him was about the same.

Gray shut the door. So much for discretion. This would probably end up in a tabloid next week. *Rockstars engage in night of debauchery.* Maybe they should break a lamp or two and throw a couch out the window to squeeze maximum juice from the story.

He headed into the bedroom, stopping dead at the sight of Jazz wearing only her unclasped bra and standing in front of the window with the glitzy landscape of San Francisco stretched out behind her. "Beautiful," he murmured, dropping the bag at his feet and striding forward to grip her arms.

"The view? Yeah. I know—"

His mouth crushed down on hers, cutting off her words. He fisted his hands in her hair and stroked his tongue between her lips, snatching her breath and the moan that escaped. He wanted everything. Every sound she could make, every involuntary movement. He wanted to taste her sighs, revel in her complete loss of control. Knowing damn well she couldn't—wouldn't—lose control that way with anyone else.

He backed her up and worked to undo his jeans and boxers, not thinking about anything except maintaining the contact of their mouths and getting inside her. Nothing else existed. Molly could've walked into the room and he wouldn't have been able to stop from lifting her up and pressing her shoulder blades into the window. She gasped from the temperature difference between her body and the glass, fueling his urgency as he spread her thighs. It didn't require thought to aim. He just surged upward and she was there, a velvet fist, closing around him, trapping him in the oblivion of her slick pussy. One thrust and the frustrating day disappeared. It was all about them now. The way it had always been meant to be.

She clutched his shoulder and his hair, pulling, twisting. Rocking against him in the rhythm that belonged only to them, one they'd never had to try to find. It was as if it had always been there, waiting. This heartbeat between them, pounding faster, faster. Her breath caught and turned into a whimper. She squeezed him inside her, so tight he swore he'd never want to leave. Surrounding him, making him groan at the pressure of her bare breasts against his chest and her candy-flavored lips streaking over his. Moving like a blur, dragging him with her to the place he craved more than air.

Their place. *Theirs.*

Clamping a hand on her hip, he levered her higher on the glass, powering into her until he hit that spot that made her eyes go wide and blind. She cried out, the sound as sharp as the nails she sliced down his back. The flash of pain spurred him on, pushing him to go harder, deeper. Her head dropped back and he pulled his mouth from hers to nuzzle her neck, warming the area with soft, wet kisses until a tremor went through her again and he bit down, wresting another whimper from her throat.

Without mercy, he pummeled her against the glass, knowing he should hold back, trying to at least cushion the blows from his hips with his hands between her ass and the unforgiving window. But he couldn't stop. She ripped something from him, an emotion he couldn't tame if he tried. She was his life, and he'd die chasing this bliss with her. Into the sunset and beyond where only her fingers fumbling for his could reach him in the madness where he'd descended.

The madness of her and him, together. Finally.

He drew back and launched forward once more, his hands shaking while he tried to hold on while she struggled to lift her dark, sooty lashes. The moment their gazes connected, locked, he gave in to the unrelenting heat building inside him, letting go with a rush that drove his lips back down to hers. She offered him her breath and he took it, filling his taxed lungs with the oxygen she panted into his mouth.

Sweaty, victorious, somehow laughing like loons, they slid down the glass until they puddled on the floor. Her in his arms, still. Always. She dropped her damp forehead to his and wound her arms around his shoulders, trembling around him. *With* him. He clutched her tightly, wondering her if he'd ever be able to release her again.

Eventually she brushed a lazy kiss over his chin. "What's in the bag?"

He chuckled as he tugged her bra down her shoulders. He'd been so wild for her he hadn't even taken the time to push it all the way off. "Horny little thing."

"Duh." She swiveled her hips and embedded him even deeper inside her, causing him to grunt.

Christ, she was going to have him hard and ready to go again in no time if she kept flexing around him like that. She was soaked and hot, and knowing he'd gotten her that way in record time urged his still-simmering desire back to life.

"Go see for yourself." He patted her ass and she got to her feet, wavering just enough to make him laugh. He didn't need drugs to feel high around her. She was the sweetest fix he'd ever known.

She crossed the room and grabbed the bag then climbed on the bed to dump out his purchases. Kneeling in the center of the mattress, she laughed and gasped and muttered to herself about each item she discovered. Watching her obvious fascination made him harder and harder until he had to move or risk being permanently stuck on the floor. With an erection like he was sporting, he couldn't waste a moment.

"So what's first?" he asked, running his tongue along the inside of his lower lip as he steeped himself in how she looked. Tumbled dark hair, flowing everywhere. Ruby red nipples, winter pale skin except where his lips and hands had marked her. That heart-shaped butt wiggling while she ripped open packages.

She sat back and placed her hands on her thighs. "Um, everything?" She tugged out a thin flat item that had gotten lost beneath the rest and lifted an eyebrow. "A blindfold?"

Without responding, he went to her and removed it from the package. He waited for her to balk, to suggest they try something else first. No matter how close a couple was, a blindfold required serious trust, and God knows he'd given her reason to be wary toward him since they'd gotten together. Not for sexual reasons, but trust was trust, and couldn't be turned on and off like a light. But rather than hesitate, she brushed her hair back over her shoulders and bent her head, making it easier for him to tie it on.

Her reaction made his chest constrict as he covered her eyes with the swatch of black silky material. The blindfold had been included in a section of "implements of sensual torture" like floggers and paddles, items he'd automatically overlooked. He wanted to watch her come undone, not put more marks on her luscious body. At least not now. They were both open-minded. Someday they might explore in that direction, when she wasn't pregnant and he wasn't already on edge about hurting her.

"Lock the door," she said, and it reminded him they weren't truly alone. Molly could come back anytime.

He obliged her then returned to the bed. Without waiting for him to ask, she settled back against the pillow, the legs she spread for him so willingly shaking with a fine tremor. He steadied her with a hand on her thigh before giving in to the craving for what was between her legs. Bending his head, he took one long, slow lick, tasting them mixed together before returning for more. Her nails scraped the back of his neck as she bowed up and parted her thighs even more, not hiding her urgency at all. She loved for him to do this to her.

Almost as much as he loved it.

Grabbing her ankle, he pulled her out flat on the bed and quieted her squeal by covering her dripping pussy with his mouth. One stroke of his tongue and she was writhing, the heartbeat against his lips throbbing frantically. He drew her piercing between his teeth and lightly tugged, making her bow up from the mattress.

"How fast can you come for me?" he breathed, and she whimpered, a sure sign it wouldn't be long.

He'd let her have one more quick release before he took her up slow and let her fall.

Pushing two fingers inside her, he rubbed that swollen area that drove her wild in determined circles. He wouldn't stop until she drenched his face. All that need pouring out, flooding his mouth. Wetting his lips so that when he kissed her, she could taste what he had.

"Gray." The cry broke from her as he pumped his fingers deep. "Just like I used to imagine..." He stopped and she whimpered again, the sound pure plea.

"Imagined when?"

She whipped her head from side to side, a flush darkening her from her cleavage to the apples of her cheeks. So fucking sexy. He leaned up to nip her breast and she moaned. He knew she was probably itching to take off the blindfold so she would be able to tell where he intended to land next, but he was enjoying having her at his mercy too much. Her compact, lithe body and full, rounded breasts—even more rounded lately—and arousingly curved belly could keep him busy for a lifetime.

"Tell me."

"Back at your parents' house. When I was in bed at night...I'd think about you doing this to me."

He turned his head and lapped at her other nipple until it stood in a taut reddened peak. Then he sucked it between his teeth and her hips jerked, her pussy tightening around the fingers he still inched in and out at a pace meant to prolong, not finish.

"Then what did you do?"

"Do?" Her obvious confusion would've made him smile if he hadn't been so deadly serious about his task.

"Do. Tell me, baby."

The way she stilled told the tale, but he wanted to hear it from her pretty pink lips. In lurid detail.

His fingers swiveled as his thumb toyed with her piercing and she quivered, on the verge of soaking him the way he wanted. But not yet. Not even close.

"I'd touch myself and pretend it was you. Your fingers, opening me up. Exploring me the way I had to do to myself to ease the ache. The way you'd do to those girls in your room." She sucked in a shuddering breath, causing her breasts to rise and fall. He licked his way between them up to her throat and the guitar pick necklace around her neck, continuing upward to her ear.

He didn't have to tell her to continue, she already was.

"I'd have to try to be quiet. It'd get so hot in my room, and I'd push my covers down and imagine you walking in to find me with my hand in my panties, stroking myself." She blew out a breath, her shoulders shaking. "I'd push my finger in hesitantly at first, then harder, deeper until I had to bite the pillow to stop from moaning out loud. When I couldn't take it anymore, I'd slip another one in and think of your tongue on my clit, just licking and licking until I...oh God."

"Mmm-hmm. Finish it off," he said against her ear, his fingers tracing inside her in long, slow pulls. His thumb circling her clit and piercing while she started to quiver.

"I'd get my panties so wet. And the sheets. I'd come tasting your name, and it wasn't ever enough."

He shifted his head and spoke against her lips, moving them with his own. "What would make it enough now?"

"You. Your cock inside me. Please." She gasped between each word.

Suddenly nothing sounded better. He'd wanted to tease her with the toys, take his time. But they'd have a lifetime to explore, and he couldn't wait a second longer.

"Roll over on your side," he said, shifting behind her and slipping his damp fingers out of her slit.

She made an impatient noise as he trailed them up her belly and helped her into position. Brushing kisses over her shoulder, he reached up to tease her distended nipples with his wet fingers. Her breasts were so sensitive now that with a few flicks, she was rolling her hips in eager circles.

"I used to fantasize about you too. But it wasn't right. You were my sister."

"I was *never* your sister," she declared hotly, and he chuckled and drew her earlobe between his teeth. Tugging until she gasped.

"Didn't stop me from jerking off in the shower and imagining you on your knees in front of me. Those pretty lips open." He grazed them with the pads of his fingers. "Open up, baby. Taste us."

She sucked his fingers inside and made a sound of delight that seemed to reverberate through her body into his.

"Then I'd go into my room and I still wasn't done. I'd grab a T-shirt and walk to the walk between our rooms and wait until I heard your voice. You'd laugh, and I'd have my hand on my cock. Pumping it into my fist, stroking so hard that I soaked my shirt." He pushed his fingers deeper into her mouth and she sucked harder, right up to the knuckle. "You never knew how I wanted to fuck you back then, even though it was wrong. I wanted to be your first. Your only."

Rather than speak, she shifted her leg up on both of his, spreading herself open for him. She knew that was an invitation he could never refuse.

But first, he had something to take care of.

He reached across her belly, the light pressure of his arm causing her to squirm. He grabbed a thin wand vibrator, the kind that would never satisfy her on its own. That's why he'd chosen it. This would rev her up, and he would help her over.

"What're you doing?" Her voice sounded muffled, thick. "I ache."

"I know. It's about to get better." He flipped the switch and the low buzz triggered her shiver. She backed into him, rubbing against his cock, and he turned his grin against her throat. "How much can you take?"

"Nothing. Not one thing."

Now he did laugh, helplessly. Her honesty at all times never failed to humble him. "You underestimate yourself, baby. But I never do." He pressed the toy against her clit, careful to avoid the piercing, and she released a high, thin cry. "Careful," he murmured against her hair. "Someone might hear you."

"Let them," she gasped.

"Naughty girl." He nipped along her jaw, drawing in the vanilla and watermelon scent he'd loved since he was a teenager. She was summer and happiness and the life he'd always dreamed of, all wrapped into one. "Tell me what you want. Beg for it and I'll give it to you. Anything you want." *Everything.*

"Inside me. Please. Now."

CHAPTER SEVEN

The man she loved was a sadist. How she'd never known this fact before she pledged to live with him for the rest of her life, she did not know, but boy, the knowledge was cold and cruel now.

He gave her what she asked for—sort of. He slipped something inside her, but it wasn't his cock. The toy was so narrow that even her most vigorous clenching didn't begin to alleviate the emptiness. She rocked upward, desperate for more, and he only grazed his teeth down the side of her throat while he bumped up the setting higher and higher. Until she clasped the sheets in sweaty hands and mumbled pleas she wasn't even sure he could understand.

"I know. I know what you need, sweetheart."

Somehow he was on the move again and she felt his mouth between her legs, playing with her piercing, taunting her clit, as he pumped the vibrator in and out. That wicked tongue stroking, licking. The pleasure tightened inside her, coiling hot, leaving her helpless to stop writhing while he drove her up to the cliff and left her hanging there.

And then when she was absolutely certain she couldn't hang on another second, he replaced the vibrator with his thick, throbbing cock and shoved her into freefall.

"Come with me," he whispered into her mouth, drawing her up into his arms. She still was, couldn't stop. She shivered with endless spasms, incapable of doing more than holding on to him and moaning from the incredible assault on her senses. Only the feeling of him rearing back and slamming home one last time before he spilled himself inside her registered through the haze.

Afterward, he pulled off the blindfold and she blinked against the bright light of the suite. For a second, she marveled at how easy it was for her to get naked with him now, whether in full light or bright sunlight. No part of her was off-limits to him. He had her trust and her heart and her soul.

"Sleep," he said against her cheek, and she was already nodding and curling into the silky sheets. Her body felt wrung out in the best way possible.

He turned off the light and rolled into the bed behind her, pulling her close. "Love you. So fucking much."

Her lips curved. She couldn't even admonish him for the curse when he swore like that. It was probably his way of bending the rules. "Love you more," she murmured, lacing her fingers with his over her belly.

His warm breath on the back of her neck lulled her into rest. Just a nap. It wasn't that late yet and they had so much to explore. She'd barely checked out the suite and God, they were in San Francisco, her favorite place in the universe.

The place where she'd be getting married. Tomorrow. With her best friend and her band and her sister—God—all in attendance. Her life wasn't anything close a fairy tale, but right now it was doing a damn good job of resembling one.

Her bladder woke her. Naturally. She ignored the urge to pee for as long as humanly possible, and rolled over with a groan, pressing her face into bedding that smelled of Gray's spicy aftershave.

Smelled of him, but he wasn't there. His side of the bed was cool.

She shoved her hair out of her eyes and leaned up one elbow, squinting as she got her bearings. This wasn't home. They were in San Francisco, at the Palatial hotel. In the tricked-out, impossible to believe penthouse suite. Sunshine trickled through the window, bathing her in a warm glow.

Morning already. Damn, she felt wasted, and she'd had nothing stronger than great sex.

She glanced around, taking in the antique furnishings and expensive trinkets that seemed to be everywhere. A crystal dish of mints on the nightstand. A cut glass water pitcher. A bunch of sex toys littering the thick cream rug.

A laugh escaped her. Oh yeah, they'd ordered sex toys instead of a late night snack. Hard to forget that.

And they weren't alone. Her *sister* was with them. The girl who just happened to be screaming like a pissed off banshee in the next room.

Screaming was probably an overstatement. Slightly. Now and then low male tones that Jazz swiftly identified as Gray's voice calmed down the screeching, only for it to start again along with the clinking of bottles. Someone was drinking. Maybe they both were.

Jazz shook her head. Stupid. Gray had never been much of a drinker, and he definitely didn't touch the stuff now. Clearly she needed to head into the bathroom and take care of business so she could figure out what was going on before they killed each other.

She climbed out of bed and glanced around for her clothes. They seemed to be strewn in places other than where she'd left them, but she picked up her shorts, bra and shirt and headed into the bath. She'd change after she spoke to the combatants in the next room. It was her wedding day, so that meant she should—

She stopped and stared at herself in the mirror, barely noticing the smudges under her eyes or the wild bedhead. All she could think about was one word.

Wedding.

Wedding.

Holy-fracking-hell-wedding.

A wedding meant she would be married. An actual adult with actual responsibilities beyond taking care of herself. She'd gotten the first heads up that things were changing in that department when the pregnancy test came up positive, but this was a whole new ballgame.

This was the first day of the rest of her life.

At the renewed sounds of fighting in the other room, she sighed and hurried up. The first day of the rest of her life was starting like many of the days prior—with squabbling before breakfast—though the players were different. Nick wasn't bitching about someone eating his cereal and Simon wasn't laughing as Deak told him to put on some damn pants. She was used to those sounds. Heck, she even enjoyed them most days. The argument in the living room had a decidedly different tenor.

She washed up and pulled on her clothes, then stopped at the bathroom door. Something made her hesitate before pulling it open, and her lack of movement made it easy for her to hear Molly's latest declaration.

"No money's enough to stay to listen to this bullshit."

Jazz wrapped her fingers around the knob, her spine turning to ice. Goose bumps popped up on her skin and she tightened her grip to keep her from swaying on her feet.

It couldn't be what it sounded like. Molly was just spouting off, as Jazz could already tell she did regularly. She shouldn't read more into it. What she needed to do was walk out there, tell them both to shut up, and find out what exactly was going on.

"Keep it up and you won't be getting any."

Jazz shut her eyes at Gray's hushed voice, incapable of smothering the pained noise that escaped her. He was trying to be quiet, so she wouldn't hear. His wife-to-be, the woman he loved enough to arrange weddings for without her say and pay off her estranged family members so she could pretend he had a normal family for one day.

She'd had enough pretenses for one lifetime. Probably two.

You wondered why she came with you. She hated you on sight, and now you know why. She'd intended to do just what Harper thought, but for some reason she changed her mind and then she wanted you gone.

Jazz dropped her forehead to the door, dimly aware of their voices in the other room. Nothing could be louder than the voice in her head.

Gray decided to make nicey-nice for the wedding—no matter what it cost. That money he's been working his ass off for, taking him away from you, is now funneling into your sister's pocket so she can tolerate one day in your presence.

She was so fucking naïve. Harper was right. Hell, she'd been too dumb to see Gray was on drugs for how long? Obviously burying her head in the sand was her favorite pastime, and she'd done the same damn thing with Molly.

Now Gray was trying to smooth things over, to make sure his investment stuck around for the full twenty-four hours. How many more songs would he have to write to make up for what he'd shelled out today? What was her baby sister's asking price?

Whatever she'd demanded, he'd obviously thought the price was fair, because hey, they had a wedding to put on today. Anything to make it seem like everything was perfect for gullible little Jazz. Somehow she was supposed to smile and pledge her life to the man she adored while knowing he'd paid off her own flesh and blood.

God, how could she face Molly again? How could she face *him*? Clearly he'd already decided she needed to be coddled and protected from reality and they weren't even married yet.

So much for being partners. For sharing a life. She hadn't had a father, so he'd taken it upon himself to shelter and guide her because she was too dumb to face life as it came.

Swallowing the lump that tried to form in her throat, she turned in the knob and went back in the bedroom. After toeing on her shoes, she grabbed her purse. Once she'd ascertained that she had some money and her cell phone, she slipped out the door from the bedroom to the hallway she'd noticed yesterday. Apparently fancy suites came with more than one exit.

She'd just never expected to need to use it.

Gray was almost at the end of his rope. And when he reached it, he was pretty sure he'd wrap it around Molly's scrawny neck and pull.

How could one teenager be so damn annoying?

He'd awakened about an hour ago after a very erotic dream starring his fiancée—who had been snuggled against his chest while he had said dream—only to find Molly sprawled out on the couch in the sitting area with an array of bottles from the minibar strewn around her and some kind of dirty movie on the TV. She'd claimed it wasn't porn, though he never would've been able to tell judging from the sex act he'd walked in on.

She hadn't even seemed properly ashamed to be caught drunk and watching almost-porn. At seventeen, if his parents had caught him in such a state he would've blushed down to the soles of his feet. Not Molly. She'd just offered him a bottle and announced he'd arrived in time for "the good part."

Her reaction to his demand he pour out the rest of the alcohol—what hadn't already reached her bloodstream anyway—and change the channel had been met with an array of angry statements, ranging from "you're not my father" and "why don't you go fuck my sister again?"

If he'd had to deal with Molly before Jazz's pregnancy, he might've viewed the whole thing a bit differently. Less than a day spent in Molly's company and he was seriously doubting his ability to be a father. He had to hope his kid wouldn't be the devil spawn Molly seemed to be more often than not, but he wasn't at all certain. Perhaps it was just part of the deal. Maybe parenthood meant wading into the hellfire without a flame-resistant suit.

Before yesterday he'd been fairly confident he could handle what came his way. Now? God, he so wasn't ready.

Eventually he'd won the war of cleaning up the alcohol and turning off the TV, but Jazz's sister's mood hadn't approved after her toys had been taken away. She'd alternately sulked and pouted and screeched, nearly driving him out of the room several times. Not that she'd been willing to let him leave. She seemed prime to fight, and because he wasn't at all sure of what she'd do while unattended—she claimed to be in a band, so trashing the suite wasn't out of the question—he'd stuck it out and tried to calm her down. And shut her up.

So much for that.

Now the night had bled into day and his plan to spend part of the morning spooning—and forking—with Jazz had gone up in smoke. Molly was still on a tear, and he couldn't think for all the ranting.

He wanted a drink. A toke. Hell, a line. He fought not to acknowledge those desires, tried to pretend they didn't even exist. But Molly seemed to bring them out in him. The scent of pot clinging to her clothes hadn't helped on that score either.

The last thing a recovering addict needed was to be confronted by alcohol and weed. Not that he'd ever be able to appeal to Molly that way. She'd probably just wave her lit joint in his face and laugh.

He'd finally had enough. Molly seemed to want to burn off her aggression by picking fights with him, and he wasn't going to help her. This was his motherfucking wedding day. If she kept it up, he'd tell her flat-out—no, he wasn't paying her a dime, and she could find her own way back to San Jose, because her sister was way better off without someone so toxic in her life.

"I'm not even sure you're her sister. You could be a liar. You certainly don't share any of Jazz's good traits, and my lawyer hasn't yet gotten back to me to tell me if that birth certificate is the real deal. So you want to leave? Go." He pointed to the door. "I won't stop you."

Sympathy niggled at the base of his spine when she burst into frustrated tears and curled up in the corner of the couch, once more doing that Jazz thing of tucking her legs into her chest. In truth, that was the only proof he needed that they were sisters. They both had tempers, and they both had huge blue eyes that could brim with laughter or well with tears at the drop of a drumstick. They both giggled like twelve-year olds, joy seeming to shake them from the inside out. He supposed it made sense that their misery could be just as complete.

"You don't believe me? I gave you my birth certificate and you sent it off to some l-lawyer?"

"Why should I believe you? You admitted you intended to try to con my fiancée."

"I did not admit that. You just assumed."

"Was I wrong?"

She swiped at the tears dripping off her chin, tinged blue from the crap she'd caked around her eyes. "You don't understand what it's been like for me. Jazz got out. She got away from that bitch."

"*Got out*? 'That bitch', as you called her, put Jazz into foster care at twelve. She chose to keep you. She didn't want Jazz anymore. So you can quit the woe-is-me bullshit, because—"

"You have no idea what I've been through," she whispered, her eyes dark and desolate. "So don't pretend you know anything about me or my situation. The difference between me and my sister is that no one is coming to save me. I have to save myself."

Her words and the emotion behind them pulled at his gut in spite of his attempts to harden himself against them. Against her. She was a swindler, the kind that lured people in with their expert manipulation skills and then spit them back out before they were any the wiser. He didn't need that shit. Jazz sure as hell didn't. She was pregnant and the last thing she should have in her life was additional stress.

But Molly was her sister, he'd stake his life on it. And her sobs made him fist his hands at his sides before he chanced sitting down beside her on the fussy antique loveseat. "You don't have to be alone any longer."

She only cried harder, resting her face on the arms she crossed over her knees. Bangle bracelets and an assortment of cuffs covered both wrists, right up to her forearms. She jingled when she walked, like a oversized fairy. One thing she didn't have in common with her sister was petiteness, that was for sure.

He reached out to touch her hair, fully expecting her to turn her head and bite. Instead she crawled across the cushion and curled into his arms, crying like a lost little girl.

"It's okay," he said, awkwardly patting her back. "Everything's going to be fine."

"N-no, it's not. It won't ever be. I don't have a place to live. I don't even have a b-boyfriend anymore."

"Your boyfriend wasn't doing you any favors. You're too young for one anyway. Worry about getting yourself straight first."

"I'm not too young." She lifted her head and looked up at him out of unfocused eyes. "You have no idea what I'm into."

"No, and I don't want to." He started to nudge her back. She was staring at him a little too fixedly, her expression that of someone missing about three-fourths of her faculties thanks to alcohol. Perhaps more. "I'm going to check on Jazz. I can't believe she hasn't come out yet—"

"No. Wait." Molly licked her lips and sidled closer, sliding her hand up his chest. "Let's keep talking."

"I don't think so. I think we've talked enough." He grabbed her wrist, barely avoiding a collision as she launched an attack with her mouth. If he hadn't turned his head at the last second, she would've kissed him. "What the fuck are you doing?"

"Kissing you." She pressed against him. "You know you want me to."

"No, I damn well don't." Shaking his head, he shoved her all the way back and rose. "Look, I know you're drunk, but what you just did—not cool. In any sort of way. Surely even people like you have some kind of honor code. Screwing around with your sister's guy has to be breaking it."

Her eyes flashed. "People like me? What's that supposed to mean? You calling me a whore too, like Junior did?"

"No," he said quickly. "I would never."

"I don't need a fucking code." She sat back and crossed her arms in disgust. "Damn boy scout. I didn't realize you were completely pussy-whipped. You've been to rehab. You know how it is. Not everyone's perfect like cute, adorable little Jazz."

He threw back his head and laughed. "She's so not perfect. You have her pegged so wrong."

"Yeah, right."

"Believe me, she has flaws, and she'd be the first to admit them. Just like I do. She'd admit mine too, and you wouldn't even have to ask." His laughter subsided into a smile as he shook his head. "But she's perfect for me, and I'd like to hope the opposite is true too. So even if I didn't think you were hiding a forked tongue, I wouldn't be interested. And we both know you're not interested in me either. You just don't want to face—"

"What am I not facing?" she demanded.

"That your sister actually wants a chance to love you," he said quietly. "That maybe, just maybe, she doesn't want anything from you but you."

She turned her face away from him, effectively ending the conversation. Her soft sobs told him well enough that he'd finally reached her, deep down under all the scabbed-over layers of mistrust and rage. Whether she'd truly take his words to heart was anyone's guess.

He headed toward to the closed connecting door to the bedroom. Right now, she wasn't his priority. Jazz should've been up and moving around by now. She slept like the dead, which was why he hadn't worried too much about her overhearing their argument. He'd tried to keep Molly's voice down, but it had been almost impossible. And every damn time he'd attempted to walk away, she'd sucked him back into the conversation.

Not again.

Pushing open the door, he peeked inside and found the bed unoccupied and unmade. She must be in the bathroom. He knocked on it and when he received no response, nudged it open. Though it was obvious she'd been in there recently from the toiletries on the sink, the room was empty.

He frowned and pivoted to study the room. The doors to the balcony were closed. Where the hell was she? He glanced around, looking for her purse and her cell phone. Last night she'd set them on the dresser, but they weren't there now.

"Fuck," he muttered, striding to the room's other exit. Why did a frigging bedroom need an exit? Normal hotel rooms didn't have more than one.

So she'd have a way to get away from you.

Ignoring the voice in his head, he yanked open the door and glanced up and down the hallway. He hadn't really expected to see her hanging out by the elevator, and he wasn't disappointed.

"Molly," he roared, stepping back into the room and slamming the door.

Naturally she didn't answer.

Why the hell was he bothering with her? She wouldn't care if her sister was gone. She'd probably do a freaking jig.

He rushed through the room, checking every possible surface for a note. Nothing. He dug out his phone and searched for a missed voicemail or text, but the only texts were from Lila, reminding him of the many things he owed her for her going above and beyond today. Yet again she mentioned the book.

What book, she still didn't specify, and at the moment, he was too out of his mind to care.

Goddammit, what had she heard? That was the only explanation for her disappearing act. She would never just walk out without leaving a note behind. So Molly's shrill voice must've carried more than he'd thought. He'd been under the impression that these walls had at least minimal soundproofing, but that had probably been false advertising. Yet another way to justify stripping his wallet.

He locked his hands behind his neck and kicked the dresser with his bare foot. The pain screamed through his toes and up into his ankle and he barely even noticed. All he could think about was how much pain Jazz must be in to have willingly walked out the door and left him.

It's only temporary. No matter what she heard, you didn't come this far to lose her now.

No universe could be that cruel.

He dropped to his haunches and bowed his head. She'd never left him, not even when he'd admitted to her he was addicted to coke. Not even when he'd been beat all to shit after a run-in with the dealers he'd owed money to. She had always, always been by his side. Now on the most important day of their lives, he'd driven her away.

"Where is she?" Molly asked softly from the doorway.

"I don't know." His voice came out thick and remained that way no matter how many times he cleared his throat. "She didn't leave a note. She just left."

"She heard us."

"Good guess." He rose and turned around to stare blearily at the pastel watercolor of the Golden Gate bridge on the wall. God, he hadn't even gotten a chance to enjoy the suite with her. They hadn't gone sightseeing to the bridge and wandered over to Fisherman's Wharf as they always did when they were in town.

Rather than show her the romance he'd promised himself he would lavish her with, he'd ordered a bunch of sex toys and they'd ended up sequestered in the suite. Then he'd left her sleeping in bed to argue with her sister about the ridiculous scheme he'd enacted to try to make this day as special as possible for Jazz. Paying off Molly. Really? That was his idea of a smart move?

No wonder she'd walked out on him.

"Do you think..." Molly trailed off and stared down at her bare orange toenails. Only now did he notice her choice of pajamas—a silky cami and short set that would probably verge on indecent if she bent the wrong way. He simply hadn't looked at her that closely. No one other than Jazz ever stole his attention. "Do you think she heard me come on to you?"

The thought made his muscles lock. "If she did, you're going to explain exactly what happened. You're going to tell her how you threw yourself at me after every other way of manipulating me failed to get your desired result. That result being me handing over the cash before you realized you actually give a shit about someone other than yourself."

She cupped her elbows and said nothing. A very wise choice on her behalf, because he wasn't at all sure of his reaction if she kept talking.

He'd already heard enough from her for a lifetime.

"You're going to help me find her," he said as the haze of fury in her direction finally began to clear. What good would it do to get pissed? He needed to talk to Jazz. That was his only focus.

She nodded, surprising the hell out of him. "Where do you think she might've gone?"

"I have no fucking clue." He stalked to the dresser and picked up the car keys. "She doesn't have transportation and I don't know how much cash she had on her. She's going to be hungry—" His voice broke and he braced his fist on the wood until he was sure he could speak. "She always eats early now."

"She's okay with the baby, right? I mean, she doesn't take any medication or whatever."

"She's as healthy as a horse. So's Dylan."

"Dylan?" Molly whispered. "That's his name?"

"Not sure yet. I mentioned it. She's mulling it over." He let go of the keys digging into his palm. "Dylan Edward Duffy."

"Hmm. Do you know those initials spell DED?"

He narrowed his eyes at her and decided not to respond to her question. Murder was still against the law, last he checked. "I need to go find your sister."

"You don't know where to look. Why not just call her, ask her to come back?"

"Oh, gee whiz, why didn't I think of that? Maybe because if she left without leaving word she's probably pissed and hurt and who knows what else and won't respond just to a text."

"Let's see. Gimme your phone."

She sighed and headed into the next room, returning with her cell in its bright pink, blinged-out case. Her thumbs danced over the keys as she texted something that would probably harm more than help.

"Well?" he demanded.

"Slow your roll. Give her a minute." Her phone dinged and she smiled triumphantly before she checked it. "See?" She glanced down and frowned. "Oh. Well. That's not good."

"What?" He rushed to her side. "What is it?"

She held up her cell, allowing him to see the three words written there: *Go. To. Hell.*

"You should try," she suggested while he paced to the window and back.

About sixteen times.

"Oh yeah? And what good would that do? She's obviously got a head of mad going toward both of us." Mad he could deal with, but the hurt that must be behind it made his gut knot up like a pile of ropes. "At least she's okay. She's fine," he said under his breath, reassuring himself more than her. She probably didn't even need reassurance, since she saw Jazz as a meal ticket and not much else.

Only because she wouldn't let herself. Yet. He still had faith she'd change her mind, but he was rapidly reaching the point that he didn't give a shit.

"Wow, you really do love her."

"Would I marry her otherwise?"

Molly shrugged and picked at her nails. "My mama got married a couple times, and none of them were for love. That's kind of old-fashioned."

"Old-fashioned? Jesus Christ." He came to a halt and tipped back his head to study the recessed lights in the ceiling. "Look, I need to get out of here, track her down—"

His cell went off on the dresser and Molly grabbed it before he could. He growled while she read the text and responded, thumbs moving in a blur. Then she tossed it aside. "That was the band," she said dismissively. "No rooms are available. They're headed up here," she added, sauntering into the next room with him trailing her like cheap perfume.

"The band? What band? *My* band?"

"Affirmative." She went to the suitcase open on the floor next to the loveseat and pulled out two tops, turning to him. "What do you think? Yellow or blue?"

"I think you're asking for it—" He broke off as the room phone rang. Swearing, he made a grab for it. "Yeah?"

"I have Lila Shawcross, Simon Kagan, Nick Crandall and Deacon and Harper McCoy demanding access to the penthouse suite. They claim they have been permitted access. Is this so?"

"We aren't demanding anything," Lila said in the background. "We're much too civilized for that."

"You are," Nick said, speaking close to the phone. "Yo, dude, let us up."

Gray nearly smiled. "Yeah, allow them up, please. Thanks." He was about to hang up when he heard an obvious tussle on the other end of the line. "Is this okay?" Lila asked, clearly out of breath. "Will it ruin the surprise? We could probably go to another hotel."

"Hell no, we can't. Simon needs a shower. Now."

Gray shook his head at Nick snarking in the background. Nothing new there. "No, the surprise is pretty much in the toilet at this point."

"Oh no. Why? Did she figure it out?"

"Worse." He rolled his neck until it cracked, but it still didn't alleviate the tension building there. "The bride is missing."

CHAPTER EIGHT

"Hello. I need a bear."

"Great. Bear-Gram is certainly an excellent choice for you then. Any particular kind?"

"Yes." Gray nodded, though the guy on the other end of the phone couldn't see him. "A really big one."

Lila clapped her hands. "Time's running out, people."

As if he didn't know that. Gray pressed his fingertips against his forehead and focused on the voice on the other end of the phone rather than their manager. Lila had moved to the front of the room to command her troops, but he wasn't in the mood to listen to her latest scheme.

Schemes were what had gotten him into this mess. Why hadn't he just told Jazz he wanted to get married now? Why in God's name had he ever made that stupid deal with Molly he'd never truly intended to have to follow-through on?

Because he was an idiot. Plain and simple. And Jazz deserved anything and everything she ever wanted for tolerating his stupidity.

He would never attempt to limit her lunch consumption again.

"Actually, I'd like the biggest bear you have in stock," Gray decided. "How big is that?"

"Bear? What the hell is he doing?" Nick muttered to no one in particular.

"Six feet, sir. You need that delivered?"

"Six feet is perfect. Yes, can you deliver it today?"

"Surely. What time would you like it?"

Gray glanced at his watch. The day was moving faster than he wished. It was heading toward mid-morning and Jazz still hadn't returned any of his many phone calls and texts. He hadn't managed to make it out of the suite to track her down yet with all of the insanity that had erupted with the band's arrival. But he was going just as soon as he finished making sure that the suite would be ready for Jazz's return.

Buying trinkets for her felt like a waste of time, but he had to do something. He couldn't be out looking for her just yet so this seemed like accomplishing a task. Besides, it was better than the other idea that kept floating through his mind.

Digging through Molly's stuff until he found her weed stash and taking a nice long hit.

But he wouldn't do that. He'd been clean for months and he wasn't going to break that streak over a misunderstanding. A misunderstanding exacerbated by his abject idiocy.

That didn't mean that he wasn't tempted. Thinking about fighting this battle every day for the rest of his life sometimes wore him out. Not that he had any choice. Even if he occasionally wavered on his own value, his woman and his child deserved for him to be present and sober. For them he would slay any dragon, including the ones in his own head and heart.

And hey, the bear wouldn't go to waste. If Jazz hated it, they could always put it in Dylan's nursery once they actually found a house. He'd have to work double or triple-time now to be able to afford the down payment, especially after the price of this trip. Even so, the value of marrying the love of his life exceeded any cost. If Jazz ever spoke to him again.

"How about now?" he asked the Bear-Gram customer service assistant.

"You'd like the delivery now?"

"Well, as soon as possible. Please. It's kind of an emergency."

"An emergency that involves a stuffed bear." Out of the corner of Gray's eye, he saw Nick nod. "Makes sense."

"I stuffed a bear once," Simon mused. "It was just a chick in a bear costume. But man, she was fluffy."

"Don't you mean furry? If you do, stop there. I'm getting disturbing pictures in my head."

Gray tuned Simon and Nick out as the customer service rep explained the increased service charge that would result from a rush delivery. "That's fine. Just put it on my card. And a twenty percent tip. Oh hey, you do flowers too, right? And chocolate? I need both of those too."

"Sir, please hold."

Gray held. What else could he do? He was on the verge of a panic attack, and he'd never even had one to know what they were like. But that had to be what this was, because his heart was racing a mile a minute and he hadn't taken a full breath for the last hour.

"Oh Lord," Deacon said to Harper. "He must've really stepped in it this time."

"It's this," Harper said, patting Deak's belt buckle. "This area causes all the problems."

"Maybe with the two daddies-to-be," Simon said, stretching out his legs, "but some of us have that all sewn up."

"Right." Nick snorted. "The same dude that screws chicks in bear costumes. Hard up much?"

"Shut up," Lila snapped. "All of you." She circled her pale pink-tipped fingernails over her temple. "You're giving me a headache."

The Bear-Gram guy returned to the line. "All right, sir, what kind of flowers?"

"Everything."

"Everything?" Doubt tinged the man's voice.

"Not everything," Gray amended. "But I need enough to fill a penthouse suite. Or come close to it anyway. Give me really bright flowers that smell good. Don't care what kind. I also need chocolate. Lots of it."

"Sir, this is going to add up quickly. Just so you're aware."

Gray shut his eyes and slouched into the couch. "I don't care."

That was a lie. He did, and probably would even more tomorrow. But he couldn't concern himself with money now. "She's worth it."

When he got off the phone, he shoved his cell in his pocket. "Where's Molly?"

"If that's the babe with all the blond hair, she ducked out right after we got here. Smokin' ass," Nick added, whistling appreciatively.

"She's seventeen, you fucker." Gray shoved him hard enough to nearly dislodge him from the arm of the love seat. "She's also Jazz's half-sister."

"Well, that explains it."

Gray narrowed his eyes. "Now is not the time for you to talk about Jazz's ass."

"No more ass talk here." Nick held up his hands. "Damn, seventeen. That's unfortunate."

"Not for her," Lila said. "She just got the luckiest break of her life."

Gray stood. He didn't have time to worry about where Molly had disappeared to. Now that the band had arrived to hold down the fort, he could look for Jazz. He hadn't wanted to leave if there wasn't someone reliable to remain in the hotel in case she returned—and Molly did *not* qualify as reliable—but now he could go. "I'm going to see if I can find her. I'll check in soon."

His phone buzzed and he glanced down, hope surging until he saw Molly's wide grin fill his screen. She must've added herself to his contacts when he wasn't looking. "Where are you?" he asked.

"I'm looking for your girlfriend. Uh, I mean fiancée."

Yeah, right. He'd believe that when he saw it. "Oh really? How do you know where to look?" He wasn't even sure, and he would've said he knew Jazz better than anyone.

Yet he still did things he knew would cause her stress. Like setting up surprises when she hated surprises, all in an effort to show her that some could be good.

Big ol' fail whale on that one. Finding out you had been booked without your consent to marry the man who had botched your already sketchy family reunion ranked right up there with the "surprises" of chickenpox and finding a snake in your bed.

"Mama brought us to San Francisco a couple of times when I was little," Molly said, raising her voice to speak over the traffic noises in the background. "I don't remember a lot. She took us to Alcatraz once."

"The prison? Why?"

"They do tours and stuff. It's a historical thing. I don't know." A car honked. "Good luck on finding her to ask her. Last I knew she booked for the Midwest with her new dude."

He fell silent. Sometimes it was easy to forget what Jazz and Molly had come from, because he was all about the now. But he couldn't let himself forget. What they'd lived through had shaped them both.

"Where else?" he asked quietly.

"It's hard to remember. I was pretty little. I remember going to the pier and The Presidio. She loved the Yerba Buena Gardens. We both did."

His heart galloped. "Check there then. I'll meet you."

"Too late, I already did. She's not there. At least not where I can easily find her. These places aren't tiny, you know. And they get super crowded. Damn tourists."

He nearly reminded her that technically all three of *them* were tourists, since none of them were from San Francisco itself. At the moment, however, he was willing to curse about tourists too. Anything that kept him from finding Jazz.

"But don't worry. I have another idea. I'm on my way there to check it out."

"Where is it? I'm on my way."

"Stay at the hotel. I've got this. Entertain your little band friends." He could almost picture her wiggling her fingers as if she were referring to kindergarten playmates. "Especially Nick. Jeez, he's even hotter in person."

"You. Are. Seventeen. He is not. Plus I'm pretty sure he has herpes."

"If you're referring to me, I so do not," Simon called.

"Ew. Gross. Really?"

Gray started to admit he was only kidding, then decided to leave it alone. If it deterred Molly from chasing after yet another older guy, he'd keep right on lying.

More lies and half truths. The toll was climbing.

"Call me when you find Jazz," he said, clicking off.

He glanced up to find the room had cleared out except for Simon and Nick. "Where did everyone go?"

Simon shrugged and kept playing with his phone. "Lila's making calls in the bedroom. Harper went off half-cocked, determined to find Jazz on her own and Deacon chased after her yelling about 'needing a plan'. Nicky—" He lifted his head and smirked. "Nicky has herpes."

"Bastard." Nick turned toward Gray. "Did you just tell Jazz's sister I had herpes?"

In spite of everything, Gray couldn't fight his grin as he dropped onto the loveseat. He'd already nearly worn a hole in the thick carpet from pacing. "That obvious, huh?"

Nick pulled one booted foot up across his other knee. "Doesn't mean good things for you if that's true, brother."

"Oh, here we go. Back to the threesome heard 'round the world." Simon rolled his eyes. "It doesn't mean good things for me either, because hello, we dipped in the same troughs a few times too. But all the threesomes you had with me don't count. Just the one with *him*."

"I'm starting to think you boys are all a little too close," Lila said, sailing into the room, clipboard in hand.

Gray could actually feel his ears heating up. "One threesome," he muttered. "Just one. One and only for my entire life."

"I'm sorry," Simon said sincerely. "There's still time to turn it around. Don't give up yet."

"As much as I enjoy hearing about the cesspools of STDs you've all happily waded through, I think we should focus on finding Jasmine. Since the wedding is due to take place in oh," Lila consulted her watch, "approximately two-and-a-half hours."

Gray laced his fingers between his knees and exhaled. "Not thinking it's gonna happen, Li."

"Excuse me? Did I or did I not make all kinds of arrangements to help you make sure this went off without a hitch? Did I or did I not endure having to go pick up your wedding bands with this Neanderthal—" she gestured at Nick, who only smirked, "—along with suffering through a flight's worth of *un*funny toilet humor? Did I or did I not—"

"Hold it." Gray held up a hand, cutting her off mid-tirade. "You picked up my wedding bands with *Nick*, of all people?"

For the first time that he could recall in recent memory, Lila actually shifted her gaze away as if she was embarrassed. "There was a sizing issue. I needed a man's hand."

"You know, because we're close to the same size and all." Nick waggled his brows. "Except in certain notable areas."

"So your dick's tiny and covered with blisters. Sexy." Lila turned her back on Nick while Simon choked out a laugh.

"Anyway, as I was saying. I contacted your parents. I spoke to your priest and doublechecked that the venue was booked. I sent out a press release to make the paparazzi think Oblivion would be anywhere but near San Francisco today. I picked out flowers and a dress for your bride. And the list goes on and on."

Gray pushed a hand through his hair. Christ, could the boulders of guilt on his shoulders get any heavier? "I know and I really appreciate it—"

"Appreciate my ass."

"Oh, I do," Nick said from behind her, which she didn't appear to hear. Or else she chose to ignore him, as anyone with a brain did.

"My point is that I went to a lot of effort to make this happen, Grayson. It is going to, or by God, you will pay me reparations."

"Just add it to my tab. Everyone else is." Gray sagged into the cushions and stretched his arm across the back. He didn't feel relaxed at all, not one bit, but what the hell could he do? Somehow he'd wandered into a Julia Roberts movie without realizing it.

All they needed was a damn horse.

"The carousel. Really?"

Jazz stopped digging through her wallet for change for another ride on the carousel at the zoo—her inner child was eight, so what—and glanced up at the sound of the familiar female voice behind her. Great. Just what she needed when she was searching for stress relief.

The junk food she'd scarfed down without Gray to lecture her about proper pregnancy nutrition hadn't even tasted that good. All it had done was give her indigestion.

Figured.

If that wasn't enough, she'd been recognized by a pair of gawking teenagers as soon as she arrived at the zoo. Having fans come up to her was still a novelty and normally she loved talking to fellow music freaks, but when her eyes were grainy from trying not to cry and she had heartburn and felt icky from wandering around in the clothes she'd worn yesterday, she wasn't all that sociable.

She'd posed for a picture with them and signed some stuff and they'd gone away happy, so obviously she hadn't been too much of an ogre. But man, she hated feeling bitchy. Dealing with Molly right now probably wouldn't help even her out, either.

Jazz turned and narrowed her eyes. "What are you doing here?" She swallowed the bitterness in her throat. Whether it was from the corn dog she'd eaten in record time or caused by Gray and Molly's deception, she wasn't sure. "Did he offer you extra hazard pay if you added some field work to your list of duties?"

Molly sighed and propped her fists on her hips. "I knew it. I figured you must've overheard either that or the whole kissing thing. Either one was—"

"Kissing who?" Jazz snapped the hairband off her wrist to do her hair up in a quick bun and stepped toward her sister. "If you mean what I think you mean, take off your jewelry. This shit's going down now."

"Damn, girl." Molly laughed. "I didn't know you had it in you."

Growling, Jazz advanced another step.

"Ease up, pitbull. My lips did not touch his lips."

"Did they touch any other part of his anatomy? Because, believe me, that won't save you any broken bones."

"No part of us kissed, I swear. He totally shut me down. Didn't even notice my tits damn near hanging out of my top." She glanced down at her breasts and sighed. "They're good tits. Everyone says so."

"Yeah, well, he's played with the prototype model, so you're out of luck, pal."

Molly whistled. "The pregnancy thing is so working for you in that area. Not that I saw anything but magazine pictures of you before, but wow, impressive."

"Thanks. I'm wearing a good bra." Hearing herself, Jazz shook her head. It was a warm day and evidently she was already suffering the early signs of heatstroke. "Look, don't change the subject. You came onto Gray? After taking his money to spend the day with me? I mean, seriously, am I that awful?"

"No." Molly blew out a breath that fluttered her curls. "You're amazing, and that's why I hate you."

As the carousel started up behind her again, Jazz sighed and tugged Molly over to a bench some distance away from the cheerful circus music. "You realize that makes no sense, right?"

"It makes plenty of sense." Molly flopped at the end of the bench and stared at the revolving carousel horses with something akin to wistfulness, shocking the hell out of Jazz. She'd yet to see even the tiniest hint of nostalgia in her sister.

Jazz, on the other hand, still wore the first piece of jewelry Gray had given her—the guitar pick necklace from a vending machine currently around her neck—and had pressed in a book the corsage he'd bought her for a high school dance. Every note or card he'd ever sent her was tucked into the diary she'd kept as a teenager. She had all of her old yearbooks and even her band uniform from the short time she'd tried to participate in an organized school activity.

Then there were all the other ways she was a sentimental fool. Crying during Hallmark commercials was now a part of her daily routine. She lavished toys and treats on her guinea pig, Ratt, and the kitten she'd bought on a whim from a kid selling them in front of the grocery store. She'd also foisted the other two kittens on Lila and Harper, whether they wanted them or not. Already she was itching to decorate her baby's nursery—though they hadn't yet bought a house—and she wasn't due until the fall. She was a sap, pure and simple.

Yet another way she and Molly were absolutely nothing alike.

"You remember riding the carousel?" Jazz asked, unable to help herself. She was firmly stuck in sap 101, endlessly pursuing kinship with other secret saps.

"Yeah. That's how I knew to come here. I remember Mama letting us have two rides each when we begged." Molly stared at the revolving brightly painted horses for another moment. "I bet you can't wait to put Dylan on one of them."

Jazz couldn't hold back a smile. "Actually, I was already thinking about that. Wait, how do you know his name is Dylan?" Then she sighed. "Gray. Your new best friend. Of course."

"Best friend? Yeah, right. The dude hates me, as he probably should. I've been nothing been nasty to him." She swallowed hard and dragged her attention from the carousel to Jazz. "And to you."

Jazz didn't reply, just watched the horses go round and round while excited kids laughed and hollered and grinning moms and dads hovered nearby.

Someday soon that would be her and Gray. Fretting over their child's first words and first steps, applauding him for reaching the smallest milestones. Cheering him on every day of their lives.

"This is the kind of place parents should bring their kids. Mama didn't do enough of that stuff with us, even in the early days." Molly lowered her head. "I always figured that's why you wanted to leave."

Jazz nearly lost her grip on her wallet. She fumbled it back into her lap, then stared open-mouthed at her sister. "Wanted to leave? Are you crazy?"

Molly didn't look at her. "It's okay. I already know."

"Whatever you think you know, whatever she told you, it was a lie. I didn't want to go anywhere. I was twelve when she shoved me into foster care. I wanted my damn mommy. I wanted my sister." Jazz blinked back the tears that rushed into her eyes right on cue, but she didn't have a hope of stemming the tide. She'd been struggling against them for way too long. "God, I love you,

Mol. I thought of you as my baby. I used to push you around in my doll stroller when you were small enough, then I'd carry you on my back everywhere when you got bigger. You'd always yank out my earrings and I'd laugh even though it hurt." She wiped at her tears. "Do you remember any of that? Please tell me you do."

"I remember," Molly whispered, gazing down at her hands. "I remember everything."

"I never would've left you on my own. I hated being away from you. For the first year, I wrote you letters every week. I had to save my lunch money to afford stamps. But you never answered them." Jazz rubbed furiously at her damp cheeks. "You were too little, but I thought maybe you'd send back a drawing or something once in a while. But nothing ever came. Ever. I kept sending them every month anyway, right through high school. By then you were old enough to write back—"

Molly swiveled to face her, her eyes wide. "She never gave me any letters. Not one. I swear to you. If she had, I would've answered every one. Even if all I could've managed in the beginning was Strawberry Shortcake stickers and I love you."

"Looks like we were both screwed over by dear ol' mom yet again." Jazz started to say more then realized Molly was sniffling. Her mascara was running from tears. Real ones, not ones used to manipulate.

Jazz tried to speak and found she couldn't. All she could do was reach out to grab Molly's hands.

"You said love," Molly said, her throat working. "You said you *love* me, not loved. Not past tense."

"Of course I do. How could I not? You're my baby sister. I loved you from the minute Mama told me she was pregnant with you. I had one of those *I'm the big sister* T-shirts that our grandma gave me and I wore it every day." Jazz smiled through her tears. "I was so proud."

Molly laughed then released her hands. Jazz tried to take it in stride, to remember that Molly was an independent sort and a few declarations, no matter how heartfelt, weren't going to erase years of distance. Intellectually, that seemed reasonable. Emotionally, it hurt like hell.

She wanted her sister back, goddammit.

Before Jazz could figure out what to say next, Molly flung herself into Jazz's arms, hugging her so hard that Jazz gasped. Molly immediately reared back and cupped her hand over her mouth. "Oh God, did I hurt you? Did I squash the kid?"

Jazz laughed. "No. You hurt my boob, not my belly. The kid's fine." She looked down at the slight rise under her maternity shirt. "Well, pissy about today's breakfast of corn dogs, but other than that, perfectly healthy."

"Corn dogs for breakfast? Seriously? See what happens when I take my eyes off you?"

Jazz went still as that beloved deep voice sent shockwaves over her skin. She glanced at Molly, who gave her an impish shrug. "Had to call and tell him when I found you. Figured I owed him that much since I drove you away."

"You didn't drive me away on your own. You both did," Jazz said, lifting her voice though she still didn't turn her head in Gray's direction. She was no dummy. One look into those sexy gray eyes and she'd crumble like a day-old cookie. "How much did he offer to pay you to act like my sister for the day?"

Molly had the decency to seem chagrined. She ducked her head, her cheeks flaring pink. "Uh, we didn't discuss an exact price."

"Yeah, because I never intended to pay her a damn dime."

Both Molly and Jazz shifted in Gray's direction. He lifted a shoulder. "Sucks when you con a con artist, doesn't it?"

Rather than getting angry, Molly shook her head and smiled. "Should've guessed you'd be a welcher."

"I wasn't welching. I know my girl. Anyone who spends five hours in her presence falls in love with her. I figured if you had a whole day to get to know her, you'd probably end up offering to pay *me* in gratitude." He shrugged and gestured toward their linked hands. Jazz wasn't even aware of Molly reaching for hers again, but she must've. "Was I right or was I right?"

Jazz set her chin. "You expect me to believe you made a deal to pay her that you never thought you'd have to pay because she'd decide she wanted to be my sister again, all on her own."

"Yes." He faced her squarely. "I knew all you two needed was time together, and the promise of paying her was enough to get her in your sphere for more than ten minutes. She wanted us gone as soon as we got to her apartment, in case you didn't notice."

"I did notice. Talk about a mixed-up signal. Come see me, then turn around and leave."

"Because it all came flooding back when we were face-to-face. How you used to sing to me and play your guitar and write these goofy songs about playing in the mud." Molly sniffled and lowered her gaze to their joined hands. "I couldn't look you in the eye and try to become part of your life for anything but genuine reasons. And if I couldn't get money out of you, I needed you gone."

"You need cash that badly?" Jazz asked gently. Amazing how a few minutes of talking things out had smudged away the worst of the hurt. Now she was back in her natural protector mode.

"Get a job," Gray suggested.

Jazz narrowed her eyes at him. They'd so be having a conversation later.

"I have a job. I'm in a band. Didn't you see my guitar? It's in your damn trunk."

He crossed his arms and lifted a brow. "Yeah, well, I'm in a band too, so I know how shitty they usually pay. I meant a real job with an actual income. Something you earn for yourself rather than relying on whichever guy strolls through the door promising you the world and delivering nothing."

Jazz bolted to her feet. "Gray—"

"No, don't." Molly grabbed her hand. "He's right."

"He is?"

"I am?" Gray cleared his throat. "I mean, of course I am."

Jazz couldn't help grinning at the jerk. She also couldn't help loving him even more for trying to give her a day with her sister, even if his methods were all wrong. "What is this, you trying your daddy training wheels out?"

"He's right," Molly said again, tightening her hold on Jazz's hand. "I tend to trust the wrong guys. I...well, I guess I shouldn't be trusting any guys right now, period. They only want one thing."

"Especially don't trust guys in bands," Gray added. "They're fuc—freaking horndogs."

"Exhibit A," Jazz agreed solemnly, kicking her foot in his direction.

"Smart ass."

Jazz glanced at Molly and gave into the urge to stroke her silky curls back from her face. She'd always been beautiful and had only become more so with age. "You should focus on school right now, and yes, a part-time job would be good. The boy thing can wait."

"Um, I'm not exactly in school at the current time." Molly bit her lip. "I'm done."

"What do you mean you're done? It's not the end of the school year yet. You shouldn't be graduating until next year."

"I dropped out."

"What? Why?"

"Sit down," Gray said, nudging her back on the bench without waiting for her opinion on his directive. "You're all flushed. It's too hot out here to raise your blood pressure."

"It's not hot, and I'm not flushed, and my blood pressure is fine. Mol, why aren't you in school?" she demanded.

"I dropped out after Mama split last year. School is so fucking lame."

Jazz sighed and shook her head. "Guess I found one way that we're alike after all. It's not a good thing to have in common. I hated school too. Skipped all the time."

"Really?" Molly's baby blue eyes lit up. "And you turned out fine. See, school isn't even necessary. It's just a big waste of time."

"I'd like to point out that she just swore in front of Dylan and you said nothing. I detect bias."

Jazz ignored him. "I turned out fine because I ended up taking college classes and trying again even when I didn't want to. School is important for your future. You can't just assume the band thing will work out. The odds aren't in your favor. They aren't in *anyone's* favor."

"You did okay. Both of you did," she said, shifting her head to include Gray. "With an amazing example like yours, why wouldn't I think I could make it too?"

"Con. Artist," Gray said under his breath. "A good one, I'll give you that."

"You could practice with us now and then, if you wanted. Get a feel for how a working band operates. Maybe come to a show or two. If you wanted," Jazz said again, hating how tremulous she sounded.

"Really?" She glanced from her to Gray, her cheeks pink with excitement. "That'd be amazing. You're cool with it too?" she asked Gray.

He sighed heavily. "Yeah. Sure. Why the hell not."

"Thank you. This is so incredible." She hurled herself at Jazz again, who was a bit more prepared this time and managed to catch her without losing feeling in her left breast. "I'm sorry we got such a rocky start yesterday. I never should've believed Mama," she said next to Jazz's ear, low enough for only her to hear.

"It's okay. We'll figure it all out." Jazz patted her back. "We have time."

"Yeah. We do." Molly pulled back and aimed a sly grin at Gray. "Guess y'all want some alone time now. I'll just go look at the giraffes or something til you're ready to go." She gave Jazz a sheepish look. "I can catch a ride back to the hotel with you guys, right? My fundage situation is kind of sketchy at the moment."

"No kidding," Gray said. "Yeah, we'll find you."

"Great. Thanks." Molly bounded up and probably would've kept on going if Gray's voice hadn't stopped her cold.

"Wait a second." He crossed his arms over his chest again, doing his best irritated parental unit imitation. Jazz had to hand it to him. He was kind of a natural. "I believe you have something else to confess to your sister. Involving me."

She blinked at him, all wide-eyed innocence. "I do. What?" Then her face clouded and she waved her hand. "Oh. That. Yeah, we already talked about how I tried to kiss you. She's cool. You're cool, right?" she asked Jazz.

"Well, I wouldn't say cool exactly, but I'm not murderous about it, so I guess we're all good."

"You're not angry?" Gray asked, clearly perplexed.

"Nah. She won't do it again." Jazz looked to Molly for confirmation. "Right?"

Molly nodded with all the sincerity of a Girl Scout. "Absolutely not. It was just a random drunk moment. You know, total beer goggles." She waved at them and started heading toward the bright sunshine beyond the exit of the carousel building.

Jazz frowned at Molly's retreating back. "Wait a second. Beer goggles? You were drunk?"

"See ya later, sis," Molly called, disappearing into the crowd.

"Dear God. I'm not ready for this." Jazz buried her face in her hands, her shoulders shaking from laughter or disgust or hell, maybe even joy that she might, just might get her sister back again for real.

"Exactly what I said." Gray dropped to the bench beside her and stretched his arm along the back. "So how's my baby?"

"Still irritated at you."

"Even the fetus is? That's pretty impressive. I didn't realize they were capable of—" He laughed when she hit his arm. "Watch it, slugger. I've had a long day."

"You have? What about me? I thought you two were plotting against me." Saying it out loud drove home how dumb the whole thing was. Molly was still a little bit of a wild card—okay, a lot of one—but she knew Gray, heart and soul. He'd never do anything to hurt her unless he had absolutely no choice.

No one was arguing his methods needed some serious improvement. But the motivation behind them couldn't be faulted, ever. Not when one glance into the eyes she knew so well told her how much he loved her.

She might still have a case of heartburn from hell, but she was a lucky, lucky woman.

"Plotting, yes. Against you? Never." He sucked in a breath. "Though now's probably as good a time as ever to tell you that I hatched another scheme yesterday, and I suppose it serves me right that it's not going to happen."

Jazz frowned. "What do you mean the wedding's not going to happen?"

"Look at the time. We're running out of it. We still have to—" He broke off and locked his jaw. "How do you know about the wedding?" He slapped a hand against his forehead. "Christ, why am I even asking? The motormouth from San Jose, right?"

"Nope. It wasn't Molly." She shouldn't feel smug that he'd guessed wrong. Besides, she shouldn't even be having this conversation. Harper had sworn her to secrecy.

"Then who? Lila?"

"No way. Lila's like a drill sergeant. She never violates protocol."

He rubbed his jaw. "Well, then, how the hell—" He groaned. "Fucking Harper. You damn women can never be trusted."

"Hey, hey, hey." She cupped her stomach. "Little ears."

He laughed, shaking his head. "See? Biased."

"No bias. It's just the baby knows your voice. In fact, I'm pretty sure—" A sudden ripple through her stomach made her stop and rub her belly. "Huh. Weird."

"What weird? What? What's wrong?"

She grabbed his hand and placed it where hers had been. "Feel that?"

From the wrinkle between his brows, she knew he was concentrating hard. He heaved out a breath and shook his head. "No. I don't feel anything. What's happening?"

"I think the baby just kicked. Either that or I'm never eating corndogs again, because I think one's alive inside me and trying to get out."

He laughed again and slid his hand down over the slope of her belly. "No. Nothing. What did it feel like?"

"It's hard to explain." She shrugged helplessly and guided his hand back to where she'd felt the first sensation. "It feels like...that," she said triumphantly when it happened again.

"That's a kick? That ripple?"

"Well, I haven't been pregnant before, but from my reading it seems possible."

"It's early."

"Tell your son that," she said drily, nudging him back. "Anyway, if we're running late, we better get a move on. I'm not doing this twice."

But he wasn't paying attention to her any longer. He dropped to his knees between her legs and slid his long-fingered hands over her stomach, sculpting the small bump. "Hey Dylan, it's your daddy. Your mom thinks you're just a corndog. Kick her again and prove her wrong."

"Watch it," she said, but she couldn't help laughing. God, he was so cute and she was so ridiculously in love with him, no matter what bonehead moves he made or silly stunts he tried to pull off.

Except their wedding. That was no stunt. This was the most important day of her life.

"I think you're trying to let us know that you don't approve of us fighting or worse yet, your mom walking out without talking to me and making me practically sick with worry all day. So sick that I spent your college fund on bears and bouquets and enough chocolate to fill the Titanic."

"Sick with worry?" She brushed his long dark hair out of his eyes. "Really? And what bears?"

But he wasn't finished. "She was right to walk out on me though, because I was an ass—assorted names she could call me, and probably will later. I'll take them. I shouldn't have offered her sister money, even if I didn't think the bill would ever come due. I shouldn't have planned a wedding without talking to her first and getting her input, but see, the thing is, I just want to be married to her so damn bad that I don't want to wait another hour, never mind another day."

"Gray," she warned, sniffling. "I have cried enough today. I am not getting married with red eyes."

He glanced up at her. "You still want to marry me?"

"Are you fucking stupid?"

His lips quirked. "At times, yes. As yesterday and today have proven without a doubt." He lowered his head and kissed her belly button. "But I love you with everything I am and everything I hope to be, and I gotta hope that's enough."

"It is. More than." She smiled mistily and covered his hands with hers. "I shouldn't have walked out on you. I should've talked it out."

"You should have. And if you do that again, there will be punishments." His smile turned naughty. "I have a whole brown bag of things to torment you with now."

"Hmm." She pretended to think. "And I'm supposed to want to be good, right?"

"Whether you're good or bad, I'll always be waiting for you to come home."

That right there was everything. He was her home, and she was his, and together they'd build one for their child. Nothing could be better than that.

Grinning, she squeezed his fingers. "Let's go get married."

CHAPTER NINE

This was it.

Gray waited at the end of the makeshift aisle at the top of a hill in Bridges Park with his best man, who had ended up being Simon when they'd drawn straws. He didn't have a best male friend, and Simon, Nick and Deacon all qualified as good ones.

Some might wonder how a friendship had occurred between him and Nick, and he wasn't even sure himself, but he was just as happy it had ended up being Simon. Having Jazz next to him and Nick would be just too weird. And Deak...well, Deak was needed elsewhere.

Nick and Molly and Sin from Rebel Rage—who just happened to be in the area for a solo club show—sat off to the side up front, just in front of the scattered folding chairs. They were tasked with the musical accompaniment, since Gray, Simon and Deak were a little busy at the moment. So far Nick and Sin seemed to be doing the bulk of the playing, while Molly looked back and forth between them with starry eyes. Gray had yet to see her do more than pick a few notes, but she held her instrument like she was used to it and had an ease that spoke of some practice. The ability part remained to be seen.

His parents and Lila sat in the front row, along with a few assorted gawkers Jazz had made friends with upon arriving at the park. Gray smiled. Nothing new there. Father Freeley's niece was also sitting up front, excitedly bouncing in her chair. Gray hoped the priest didn't freak out when he saw the Simon's Skanks shirt. There hadn't been a lot of time for adjustments.

Evidently there had still been enough time to attract the attention of the paparazzi. At least one or two of the spectators had whipped out a notebook or camera, and Gray had seen a chopper overhead a little while ago that had made Lila shake her fist. All in all, they weren't being bothered. If Oblivion continued its rise, they wouldn't get off this scot-free in the future, but he only intended to get married once.

Gray glanced at Simon, who kept pulling at his collar and generally looking uncomfortable. Gray, on the other hand, couldn't have been calmer. It was a perfect San Francisco day without a cloud in the sky. Father Freeley had been right. From the park, you could see the Golden Gate Bridge and the bay. From this high up, it sparkled as if diamonds had been tossed upon its surface.

For a quickly thrown together wedding, it was pretty damn nice. Nick had produced a Spanish guitar to "add some flavor" to the music and everyone was dressed to the nines—including him, because thank God, Lila had thought of tuxes. Simon had the wedding bands, which weren't exactly what he'd chosen due to the supposed sizing issue but they were close.

So far, so freaking good.

"Aren't you supposed to be walking Harper down the aisle?" he said under his breath to Simon.

He shook his head rapidly. "Nope. I'm not walking anyone down any aisles anytime soon. Bad mojo. Besides, Harp has been spoken for."

"What's that supposed to—"

The woman in question appeared at the other end of the aisle and snapped her fingers in Nick's general direction. "Wedding march, please."

He saluted her and started playing, followed swiftly by Molly and Sin. And Molly actually *was* playing. Gray watched her fingerwork for a moment, impressed in spite of himself. She wasn't phoning it in. Nice to know the girl didn't blow smoke about everything.

A hush fell over the very small crowd and he glanced toward the aisle as a beaming Father Freeley joined them up front. "Don't forget to breathe," he said to Gray.

"Oh, I'm breathing just fine."

"Fucker's not even nervous. That's not right." Apparently realizing he'd just sworn in front of a man of the cloth, Simon blessed himself. "Sorry."

"No problem." Father Freeley patted each of their arms. "If a man can't swear at a time like this, when can he? Though I do think you might rethink your breathing assertion once you see your beautiful bride." He winked at Gray.

Gray swallowed thickly. *Your beautiful bride.* She was finally his. After all the missed signals and the arguments and the times when they'd been so far apart he hadn't believed they would ever be able to close the gap, he was going to marry Jazz in front of the people who mattered most.

If that wasn't a miracle, he didn't know what was.

Deacon and Harper appeared arm-in-arm at the other end of the aisle, smiling at each other before they let go of each other to extend their arms behind them. Jazz appeared from the back and stepped between them, wearing a shoulderless cream dress with a lacy bottom and clutching a bouquet of wildflowers. Their gazes met, locked. She smiled, her joy evident even from a dozen feet away. Her lips moved and he knew exactly what she was mouthing to him because he felt the echo down to his soles.

Love you.

Grinning broadly, Harp and Deak both slid an arm around her waist and the three headed up the aisle as one. Jazz had not one person to give her away, but two, and they were two of the people she loved most in the world.

With Jazz's first step, Gray's breath faltered. With her second, his heartbeat stalled out completely. God, Father Freeley must be psychic, because his chest seized like he was having a cardiac event. Not from nerves. Hell no. From absolute anticipation that this gorgeous, perfect, completely exasperating woman truly wanted to be with him.

Forever. Finally.

As she approached, the more details he saw. She was barefoot and had flowers braided into her hair. If she wore any makeup, it was too subtle to be detected. And when she moved, the dress clung just slightly to her rounded belly.

Love slammed into him hard enough to nearly knock him off his feet, and still, he couldn't drag his gaze from hers.

When the three of them reached their version of the altar, Deak took her hand and placed it in Gray's. He curled his fingers around hers and lifted them to his mouth, unsure if he'd be able to get out the vows they'd written on their way to the park. And even if he did manage to speak, he was almost certain he'd never remember a single word while lost in her wild blue eyes.

"Dearly beloved, we're gathered here today to unite Grayson and Jasmine in holy matrimony."

"Or unholy," Simon said with a quick glance at Jazz's belly before blinking innocently.

Gray grinned and tightened his hold on Jazz's hand. Holy or unholy, any kind of matrimony sounded just fine.

Father Freeley continued through the ceremony, and Gray found his attention wandering to the warmth of her pressed up against his side. To her fingers securely nestled in his. To the way her lips twitched before she recited her vows to him and how her eyes filled up when he said his to her. He accidentally forgot a whole line and she just stared blankly when the priest first asked her if she said "I do," thereby nearly giving Gray a heart attack, but aside from those few stumbles, the ceremony went off without a hitch.

Until Father pronounced them man and wife.

Jazz tapped him hesitantly on the arm. "Sorry, Father, but can you say husband and wife instead? If he's still a man, I'm still a woman."

Simon swallowed a laugh but Gray only grinned. That was his woman, all right.

"As you wish, Miss Jasmine," the priest said, smiling. "You are now husband and wife. You may kiss the bride."

Gray had his hands in her hair and his mouth on hers before Father had even finished speaking.

She laughed against his lips and clutched his lapels, crushing the flowers between them as she kissed him back to the sounds of hooting and hollering in the background. "This is real," she whispered between kisses. One might've been traditional, but it definitely didn't seem like enough.

"Oh yeah, this is fucking real," Gray said, kissing her again before she could admonish him for cursing.

They were married. Finally.

Not quite twenty-four hours into married life, Jazz had to say it rocked.

Every day wouldn't start like today had, obviously. She wouldn't wake up in the penthouse suite next to her naked new husband—okay, so technically, she hadn't awakened *next* to him, because he'd been between her legs, mouth working hard. But close enough.

She wouldn't get to make love every day while sunshine glittered on the bay just outside her window and Gray licked her from top to bottom then started all over again. A hot breakfast of bacon, eggs and wheat toast wouldn't be waiting for her every morning. Nor would she probably ever find a silver bullet vibrator beside her plate instead of a rose again.

That had been a nice touch, she had to admit.

But right now, married life meant four orgasms before getting dressed. And that seemed like an auspicious beginning indeed.

"I'm hungry. Can we stop soon?"

"Jesus, woman, I don't want to get off the freeway yet. We're making good time."

"We're making good time because you're trying to starve us to death." Jazz glanced back between the seats and looked to Molly for confirmation. Her sister looked more than a little uncomfortable wedged in the back of their small sedan with her guitar and the giant cream-colored bear Jazz had named Bret Michaels, much to Gray's displeasure. But the bear and Bret had exactly the same mouth. "Tell him you're hungry."

"I'm hungry," Molly said dutifully without looking up from her phone.

"See?" Jazz said to Gray, slumping back into her seat. "You're outvoted."

"Once Dylan's born, you won't be able to outnumber me anymore," he said, signaling for the exit.

"Oh, about that." Jazz cleared her throat. "It's probably good that you're pulling into a rest area now, because you're going to have to reprogram the GPS."

Gray shot her a suspicious glance. He'd forgotten his shaving kit so he was sporting some sexy scruff that would've earned him a roadside quickie had they not had company. "Why?"

Jazz waited until he'd parked at the rest stop before shifting toward him with a bright smile. "Turns out Molly isn't going back to San Jose. She's coming to live with us. Isn't that fabulous?"

He stared at her for so long that she began to wonder if he'd gone into a catatonic state. "Yo, Duffy." She waved a hand in front of his face, but he didn't even blink. "You in there?"

"What do you mean, coming to live with us? We don't have our own place. We share a bedroom with a guinea pig and a kitten and if we don't find a house, we'll be sharing it with a baby." He jerked a thumb over his shoulder. "Where are we supposed to stick *her*?"

"I don't take up much room," Molly offered helpfully. "I can totally sleep in a queen bed if that helps."

"Oh, can you? That would be such a sacrifice on your part. Especially considering that Jazz and I are only in a queen ourselves due to space." Gray glanced back at Jazz. "Look, I know it's probably most men's wet dream to share a bed with two sisters, but it's not mine. If that's what's going down, you two take the bed and I'll sleep in the living room."

"He didn't say no," Jazz said to Molly, giving her a thumbs up.

"He absolutely did not. Thank you," Molly squealed, rocketing forward to wrap her arms around Gray and the driver's seat. "You're the best."

"What part of that sounded like an agreement to you? Either of you," he said, glancing between them. "I just said I'd be forced onto the sofa and for fuck's sake, I just got married. Can we wait to boot me out into the living room for at least a month?"

"There, there, sweetie." Jazz patted his arm. "No one's booting you anywhere."

"Yet," Molly added darkly from the backseat, causing Jazz to laugh.

"Am I supposed to find this funny? Any of this? How can you just spring this on me without taking my opinion into account?"

"Hmm. That's a good question." Jazz tapped her nails against her lips. "It would take brass balls to cut your partner out of the decision-making process of a major decision. I can't imagine who would do that." She looked to Molly. "Can you?"

Molly shook her head solemnly. "No. I really can't."

"I knew it. This is payback, isn't it?" He dropped his head back against the seat. "You're teaching me a lesson."

"No, not really, but if thinking that gets you to say *yes* faster, then yes, yes, I am."

"Is it too late to file for divorce?" he asked tiredly.

A couple of months ago, a question like that—even a teasing one—would've made her stomach sink to her feet. Now she only smiled sunnily. "Afraid so." She lifted her hand and tapped her wedding ring. "This here says you're stuck with me and Bret Michaels for the duration."

"And your sister. Don't forget your sister."

"It's just for a little while, I promise. I'll just crash at your place until I find somewhere to stay on my own."

"What, with some lowlife loser?"

"Gray," Jazz said, rubbing his thigh. He was tense enough to snap the wheel in half. "She's not looking to hook up with any guys. Tell him, Mol."

"No." Molly lifted her chin proudly. "I'm practicing abstinence now."

"Oh Christ Jesus."

Jazz frowned and flicked his knee. "Seriously? Language."

"Right. Tell me to watch my language, and you're bringing a pot-smoking, underage-drinking trash talker into our bedroom. With. Our. Child," he enunciated.

"Uh, your child isn't born yet."

"Close enough," he snapped. "Close e-damn-nough."

Jazz sighed and pinched the bridge of her nose. To go along with her rumbling stomach, now she had to use the restroom. Desperately. Not that she dared leave these two snarling dogs on their own without a referee. "I already talked to the guys. Deak and Harper will be moving out anytime now. Once they do, Mol can have their bedroom. She'll pay rent," she added when Gray started to object. Strenuously. "She'll sleep on the living room couch until Harp and Deak are gone, then she'll be so quiet in her own space you won't even realize she's living there."

"As a mouse," Molly said.

"A mouse that pays her share of the rent, as well as buys groceries and pays part of the utilities."

"Ok—"

"And goes to school," he said, banging the steering wheel. "If you're under my roof, you're going to get an education. I got my

Bachelor's degree before I joined Oblivion, so don't give me that 'I'm in a band' BS."

Jazz gazed at him with a mixture of admiration and annoyance. He was going to make one hell of a father. She almost felt a little sorry for Dylan, because when it came to his daddy, that kid would be getting away with *nothing*.

"I have to get my GED first. I don't have my diploma yet."

"So then you take care of that first and then you enroll in college. No excuses. If you don't believe in education, then you find somewhere else to live."

"I don't have a Bachelor's degree, in case you've forgotten," Jazz put in.

"Jasmine, now is not the time."

She tried to hide her smile behind her hand as she looked out the window. He was so freaking adorable when he got like this.

"I'll go to school," Molly said in a small voice. "I promise."

"And you'll do well too."

"I'm not stupid," she said hotly. "I used to get all Bs and Cs."

"Try As and Bs this time. There's no free lunch. And you'll babysit—" Even before he got the words out, he shook his head. "No. Scratch that. You will never babysit my child."

"Our child," Jazz reminded him. "And you don't get to say that definitively."

The way his mouth curled in horror might've been amusing under other circumstances. "You want Dylan to be smoking pot and drinking before kindergarten?"

"Really?" Jazz asked softly. "You're really going to judge her about that stuff?"

Tightening his hands around the wheel, he stared out the windshield.

"I'm not a bad person. You just got the total wrong impression of me. I can do better." Molly leaned forward, nearly knocking Bret Michaels sideways. "You'll see."

"You can and you will." Gray looked up and met her eyes in the rearview mirror. "Or you're out. No second chances."

"Okay. Whatever you say."

Jazz cleared her throat as an awkward silence descended. "Mol, would you go inside and grab us a table at that chicken place? We'll be right in."

"All right." Molly didn't hesitate to scramble out of the car. She was probably eager to get away from Gray's laundry list of rules.

And they hadn't even made it home yet.

"Don't say it," he said the instant Molly went into the rest area. "I don't want to hear about how you think I'm a jerk. I have every right to—"

"It makes me so hot when you get all commanding." She undid her seatbelt and slid across the seat to press her mouth against his neck. "I wish we were alone so I could cap off this trip the same way I did our trip to Molly's," she said, punctuating her words with a long lick up his throat.

He groaned and grabbed her shoulders, edging her back. "What is this? What are you doing to me?"

"Nothing yet." His suspicion nearly made her giggle. She slid her arm under his and gripped his cock, giving it a long, slow rub. "But I wish I was. And I will for sure as soon as we're home." She turned her head and kissed his forearm above his thick gold watch. "Then when I'm done with you, I'll need you to do the same. Trying to be quiet when you're going down on me always makes me even more excited."

"Okay, hold it. I may be a man, and thereby easily controlled with the promise of oral sex—either giving or receiving—but I'm not completely insane. After the conversation we just had, you shouldn't be propositioning me."

"Second trimester." She nipped the underside of his arm. "*Second trimester.*"

"So this is some kind of hormonal thing?" he asked, shifting closer.

She hated to dim the hope in his eyes, but she was now his wife, so she was pretty sure she was legally obligated to.

"Yes. My body is primed to respond to you as a good provider for the child I'm carrying. When I return to my non-hormonally driven state, I may smack you in the head for acting like an ass when my sister's just trying to turn her life around. I'll probably remind you that you too had some difficulties, but you had people who loved and supported you and that helped you get back on track. I might also say that I've wanted to get my sister back for the entire time I've known you, and having a chance with her again makes me so happy." She licked the spot she'd just nibbled. "You know, maybe."

He slid his hand up into her hair and pulled her face close to his. Once they were nose to nose, he bit her lower lip. "You don't play fair."

"Which part wasn't fair? Offering you a thirty-minute blowjob and possibly some motorboating—" she chuckled as his eyes widened "—or the part where I said that you'd be making me really, really happy by letting my sister live with us?" She undid the top button of his shirt and caressed his collarbone. "Please specify so I don't make the same mistake again. I'm a new wife and all, so I'm just learning how this all works."

"Evil." Slowly, he dragged her lower lip through his teeth. "So frigging evil."

"Me?" She batted her lashes and laughed when he reached around to swat her ass.

"You. You're evil and crafty." He dropped his forehead to hers. "And right."

"Hey, we're all making sacrifices. I'm going baby shopping with your mother. Voluntarily." She tried not to shudder. As much as she was hoping their upcoming bonding trip would begin to heal the rift between her and Gray's parents, she realized it was unlikely that could be accomplished in one afternoon. Heck, it probably couldn't be accomplished in a *year* of afternoons, but it was a start. "No handcuffs involved."

"The only handcuffs going on these wrists," he lifted Jazz's arm and kissed the base of her palm, "are fuzzy ones I may or may have bought while we were staying in our hotel room."

Now she was shivering for a whole new reason. *Damn.*

She bit her lip and forced herself to focus on the matter at hand. "So you'll give her a chance then?"

"Yeah. I'll give her a chance." He kissed her softly. "For you, I'd do anything."

"Ditto." She reached up to stroke his eyebrow ring. The silver somehow made his eyes seemed even more steely gray. "Thank you."

"You don't have to thank me. It's your home too. As will be our house when we get it. Which we have to do, soon."

"We'll start looking this week. I'll check some things out online."

He tucked her hair behind her ears, avoiding her eyes. "You're going to have to get the ball rolling on your own. I'm sorry, honey, but I—"

"You're going to be busy with work because you spent Dylan's college fund on bears and sex toys." She nodded. "I know. It's okay. And maybe we can do some collaborations on the songwriting end of things again like old times. See if maybe *our* songs are a hit like yours have been."

"I would love to."

"And I love you for taking such good care of us."

He grinned. "The sex toys benefitted me too. Bret, not so much." He cupped her face in her hands, his grin fading. "I don't understand it. Maybe I never will."

Her heart skipped in spite of her newfound confidence when it came to all things relationship-related. She covered his hands on her cheeks. "What don't you understand?"

"I love you so much and it just keeps growing. Every single day."

"Now who's evil and crafty?" she asked shakily, pressing her cheek to his.

"Not evil and crafty. Just honest. Marrying you is the best thing I ever did."

"Maybe, but the second best thing you ever did was follow me to Nick's that night last year."

He groaned and sagged into his seat. "Are you serious? That night was a disaster."

"It was the first night in way too long that made me think you really wanted me. We bungled things afterward, but that night was the start of us. Without it, I don't know if we'd be sitting here."

"I suppose you're right." He feathered his thumb over her wedding ring. "And here is a pretty damn fine place to be."

NEXT UP is Simon Kagan's book, DESTROYED.
Oblivion's lead singer—and resident party animal—finally
faces the one that got away.
COMING MAY 12th!
PREORDER HERE

LET YOUR VOICE BE HEARD

HIT OR QUIT: After you finish UNTWISTED please consider leaving an honest review here or on Goodreads.

COME PLAY WITH US: We have a blast on our Facebook group, Word Wenches. It's all about the teasers, giveaways, music, hot guys...oh and books. Join us!

BE SOCIAL: Taryn & Cari are all over social media. Follow TARYN on Facebook & Twitter. Follow CARI on Facebook & Twitter.

GET INFORMED: Sign up for our Lost in Oblivion NEWSLETTER for contests, advanced notice on new releases & other fun.

Lost In Oblivion

the Series
SEDUCED (intro)
ROCKED (book #1)
ROCK, RATTLE & ROLL (book #1.5)
TWISTED (book #2)
UNTWISTED (book #2.5)

Coming soon
DESTROYED
SHATTERED
If you'd like more information about the series &
extras please visit www.lostinoblivion.com.

ANYTHING BUT MINE

WHEN YOU'RE GONE TRILOGY
BOOK ONE
By Taryn Elliott

Rock star Logan King has come home to Winchester Falls for the annual Summer Festival. Only this time he's hauling a helluva lot more baggage than a few suitcases and vintage guitars. His closet contains more than the usual skeletons...and if he doesn't keep the door firmly locked, someone might get harmed. The specter of what haunts him forces him to turn away from anything more than one-night-stands.

Until Izzy and her topaz eyes finally give him a reason to try again.

Since moving to town Isabella Grace has found friends and a place to belong for the first time in her life. Running the Summer Festival is the perfect way to show how important her new community is. She just never planned on a whirlwind fling with a man too used to saying goodbye. Or to fall for a guy who has as many secrets as he does hit songs.

Logan is used to protecting himself, but protecting Izzy is all new territory. With everything that matters to him at risk, he refuses to let her get hurt—even if that means he has to walk away. For her own good.

Buy it or Try it.

SHADOWBOXER

Book 1 in the Tapped Out series
by Cari Quinn

She's in for the fight of her life...with the man who only wants to be her lover.

Fighter Mia Anderson has faced the dark side of life and survived. But just getting by is no longer enough. To fund her new life with her baby sister, she's determined to beat the reigning king of the male fighters in New York's underground MMA circuit, Tray "Fox" Knox.

Tray refuses to fight a woman, until he learns Mia's tougher than anyone he has ever known. He soon realizes he wants more from her than blows and blood, and he's willing to hit below the belt to get it. He'll fight her, but if he wins, she spends the night in his bed. All night long, his rules. No tapping out.

Mia agrees, certain that he'll lose. What she doesn't realize is that Tray loves to fight *dirty*...and that this match may end up being the most important one of their lives.

Buy or Try

www.ingramcontent.com/pod-product-compliance
Lightning Source LLC
Chambersburg PA
CBHW071521170626
46811CB00007B/2923